To [handwritten inscription]
I've been... been destroyed... sometimes lonely... for making me 'me' again
Love Always,
Gracie

The Broken Girl

Lonely Girl Series

Gracie Wilson

The Broken Girl

All Rights Reserved.

The Broken Girl is a work of Fiction. Characters, names, incidents and places are used in a fictitious manner or are the product of the author's imagination. Any resemblance to actual persons, living or dead, or actual events are purely coincidental.

Copyright © 2014 by Gracie Wilson

Cover Copyright © 2014 by Gracie Wilson

Cover Design By: Just Write. Creations

Book Formatter& Designer: Leanore Elliott

Gracie Wilson

Darkness. Pain. Loss. They are all I seem to know. Every time I get ahead, another secret or event sends me spiraling. Dillon's attack has left me fighting for the things I hold dear.

Now, I have to be brave and pick up the pieces. Hearts will be shattered and love will be rewritten. Nothing is going as planned but it never has. It's time to navigate through the chaos that's plaguing my life and figure out what I want.

Everything I thought I knew is about to be challenged. Truths will be exposed. New threats will be revealed.

Promises will be destroyed and life as I know it is about to be broken…

The Broken Girl

Chapter One

You'd think after all the heartbreak that I have been through, I'd have handled those three little words better. I will admit I didn't and I'm not proud of that fact. Rushing up to the room was the most exciting moment in what seemed like a daze of devastations. After Michael's death I'd closed myself off and only really opened up again to family, except for Keegan and Jake, so you can imagine the way I'm feeling after everything that's happened in the last year. Dillon had tried to kill me. Now I believe he'd tried multiple times. He had failed, but not at the expense of others. It was bad enough that he was behind the accident that killed Michael. But it was still an accident, something I have come to realize and adjust to. He was just a scared kid who'd run a car off the road.

The events that followed that accident are unforgivable though. Even though Michael had slept with his girlfriend, it would never excuse the fact that Dillon had indeed sought me out to get back at Michael for that. He had intentionally gone out of his way to devastate me by telling me that the incident occurred while I was with Michael. Since Michael had died in the accident, he had no way to take anything from him other than the fact he'd already taken his life. Apparently, that wasn't enough. He wanted more twisted justice. So I became his new obsession. When I say obsession, I mean that in the most real way. What I hadn't known until after I'd been in the hospital a few days was that Dillon was actually sick. He was struggling with mental illness.

    His mother had asked my parents to speak with me. She assured them she didn't blame me and that she had tried to get a handle on him. After he took off, they couldn't find him. She told me she'd tried multiple times to have him committed, but this was not an easy task to do without his consent. She cried and begged me to forgive her and to try and remember him before the accident. Before the fateful accident that had triggered something neither of us knew would go this far. With one dead, myself having to be stitched up due to the damage Dillon inflicted on me, and another two in the hospital in critical condition, it's a hard subject to purposely ponder. I remember Dillon before the accident with Michael. He

The Broken Girl

was always nice and carefree. I know most people would think I'm making excuses, but I know that he is sick. For that alone, I can reason with the fact I'm now standing where I am.

It's the day of the funeral and my heart hurts in ways I never expected. I hadn't gone to Michael's funeral and I knew I had to do this, even though some wouldn't understand. Staring at the casket as the priest talks about his life, love of sports, and the love of his friends and loved ones, I see the family look to me with pity. I stand there next to Alec, who has his arm around my shoulder, holding me protectively. He doesn't let me out of his sight now even though I've told him it's over and I'm safe. But to him, all he will remember is pulling up in his car only to find me being rushed into the hospital from the ambulance. I was barely awake and I was in shock. I hadn't needed any surgery, but I'd still been kept in the hospital a few days.

When the service finishes, I walk up to put a flower on his casket and my brother follows me to do the same. When we are heading back to the car with my parents, the phone call from the hospital comes in. They are calling to tell us that Keegan has woken up. They've kept him sedated to rest and recuperate in a medically induced coma. They'd started to wean him off and now he's awake. I don't wait, I hop in the car and pretty much yell at everyone else to get in. I'm driving this time and my family is shocked. The funeral was only an hour out of Thunder Bay so we make it back to the hospital quickly. I rush up to the floor, bolting past the nurses toward his room at a ridiculous speed. All I keep thinking is Keegan's awake; I haven't lost another person I love. Nothing, however, prepared me for what happened when I rushed into the room and hug Keegan.

He looks confused and pulls back from me, looking toward my brother who has rushed in behind me. He looks so lost that I wonder if he hates me, preferring I leave and not be here with him right now. If it weren't for me, he wouldn't be in this situation and he wouldn't be lying in this bed. I go to tell him I will leave if he wants me to, but the words that come out of his mouth leave me speechless.

"Who are you?"

I feel my breath being sucked out of me and I feel my brother's hand on my back supporting me. "Key, do you know who I am?" My brother looks like he's just as lost as I am. When he gets his response, he seems to look like he saw a ghost.

The Broken Girl

"What the hell is wrong with you, Alec? Of course I know who you are."

I begin to think he was just screwing with me, but he still looks at me as if he really doesn't know who I am.

"Keegan, man, you really don't know who this is?" He's pointing to me and I can see Keegan trying to figure it out in his head. He shakes his head in defeat and I feel my heart shatter. "Keegan, this is my sister, remember?" I see his eyes light up and I get hopeful.

"Oh, shit! Of course it is. I'm sorry you just look so different from the pictures I've seen. Thanks for coming, Bec." I feel my stomach start to contract and I put my hand over my mouth to stop the limited contents in my stomach from coming up. He called me *Bec*, not Becca. Keegan looks confused and it's upsetting him because his monitors start to go crazy. "Keegan, what's the last thing you remember?"

Keegan stays quiet for a minute, clearly trying to pick his last memory from his scattered mind. "Christmas, you got me that amazing poster of that bulldog on a skateboard." At the word Christmas I stop until I realize my brother hadn't gotten him that, at least not this past Christmas.

~ 8 ~

"That was a year and a half ago, Key." I see Keegan struggling to catch his breath and I want to go to him but he doesn't even know who I am.

"Maybe we shouldn't be doing this now, Alec. Let's just go get the doctors and we can talk about this all together." I see my voice snap him out of his episode and bring him back to reality.

"But why is your sister here and why are you acting so strange about this?"

He says *'your sister'* and I think my heart is completely broken. Clearly I was wrong. I just didn't know it yet.

"Man, she's sort of your girlfriend. Has been for a while." The shock in his eyes at the words my brother has just stated feels like a knife being put through me. Trust me. I'd know. Right now I'd gladly take that real knife over this.

"You're screwing with me! What happened to me and Sarah?" My breath is sucked out of me, causing me to get dizzy. "Wait, was I in an accident?" My brother goes over everything again. The nurse soon comes in and he explains everything to her. I haven't said a word and in all honesty, I wouldn't know what to say. Keegan looks at me and I wish I'd see a spark of recognition, but I don't. All I see is utter confusion. "So I guess I'm dating Bec Potts now."

The Broken Girl

I tense and my brother goes to grab for me. I shake my head and back away. "I'm going to go get us all some food. I'll be back." I rush out the room, leaving my brother there and I run to the lobby. I sit in a chair just wishing I'd wake up from this nightmare.

"Becca! Oh my god, Becca!" I look up and see Charlotte running up to me from the front doors. I don't get up, I just sit here as she collapses next to me holding me. "I'm so sorry I missed the funeral, Becca. My flight was delayed. I was trying to get here to be with you." I look confused. I didn't even know she was coming. "I wanted to surprise you, something happy you could have and you need some of that right about now."

She has no idea how true her words were. "Why aren't you upstairs? I heard the great news from your parents when they called me after I landed." I hadn't even thought to call my parents and let them know that Keegan didn't remember the last year and a half of his life.

"I can't be up there. It's too hard." I feel her tighten around me.

"Becca, it will all be okay. I know you have a huge thing to work out involving

Gracie Wilson

your love life, but it will be alright I promise."

I shake my head so vigorously it might pop off. "I wish that were true but nothing will be the same again." I begin to weep in my cousin's arms.

"Oh no, Becca, this isn't like with Michael. It's going to be alright."

I say the words for the first time that leave me entirely heartbroken. "He doesn't remember me, Charlotte. He doesn't remember anything about me, but that I'm Bec from the photos in Alec's dorm, Alec's little sister. Worse, he thought he was still with that bitch Sarah." I get up and take off. I can't talk about this anymore. I have to go, I need to be where I feel safe.

Charlotte didn't try to stop me when I left. She knew I just couldn't deal and had to get away. I can't keep doing this; I can't keep living this life. Not like this, not without Michael, Keegan, and Jake. I just know I'm not that strong.

I'm standing outside the door and I see the nurse come by. "Hi, sweetie, you going in?" I nod but by my expression is somber. She just puts her hand on my shoulder. "He can get through it. With a pretty girl like you, there's no way he's not coming through this. He's going to move on from all of it and you will remember this as something that bonded

The Broken Girl

you." My heart is wishing I could believe her, but without me in his life Keegan wouldn't be lying in this hospital bed. I walk through the door, seeing him bruised less than the day before, but he still isn't the same. Seeing his bandages, it makes my heart sink. Walking up and sit on the bed with him, willing him to open his eyes with my mind. So I bring my legs up to line up with his so we are lying parallel in the hospital bed. Putting my head on his chest, careful not to cause him any more pain. I've done enough of that already. The tears begin to fall and I turn into his arms. "Jake, please wake up."

Chapter Two

Lying in the bed with Jake was the only place I felt safe or normal. Jake was the one person I knew would always understand me. When Jake was brought in after Dillon's attack, he was rushed into surgery and kept in the ICU. His grandmother had come because we called her. I was listed as his next of kin for some odd reason, which permitted me to be on the floor with him. When I called her, she already knew all about me. I explained what had happened in some detail, skipping the parts she didn't need to know. She came down to the hospital, but told me that he was in amazing hands. His grandmother asked me to call if anything changed. When I asked if we should call any other family, she told me if that's what he had wanted I wouldn't have been the one listed as next of kin. She was an amazingly wild and hilarious woman. As soon as I was released, I spent every night sleeping in his room with him. At the beginning, I'd rest in a chair that pulled out

The Broken Girl

next to him. Slowly, as he healed from his surgeries, I ended up in the bed with him. "Jake, I need you. You promised you'd always be here."

I hold on to Jake, wishing my proximity could wake him from this. When I was in the hospital after the attack from Dillon last time, Jake pulled me out. "I heard you the whole time, Jake. When you talked to me when I was sleeping. So I'm going to talk to you every day and hopefully you will be hearing me." I snuggle into him, ready to bare my soul. "Jake, I love you. Not like you love me, though. When we were here, you said you loved me, but you're not *in* love with me. I couldn't admit it then, but I loved you. I'm in love with you, but I will always be your best friend first. I will put aside my feelings so that I can always be your best friend and be here for you, no matter the cost. Without you I'd be lost. If you don't wake up, I just can't… I won't survive." I hear a shuffle and look up to see my brother Alec watching me.

"Becca, it'll be okay. Jake is just resting. His body needs it just like you did, when it was you lying here and Jake begging you to wake up." He looks like he wants to say something more, but isn't sure what I can handle.

~ 14 ~

Gracie Wilson

"What is it, Alec?"

He looks at me, trying to scale my emotions before continuing. "I know you are in love with Jake. I think I knew before you knew. I know you love Keegan too, but your going to have to choose one day. For the record though, I was here when Jake was making the same plea to wake you up. He's in love with you too, Becca. He's just scared of losing you if you don't choose him. If I was him, I'd rather have you in my life as my friend than not at all." I'm shocked by this, because Jake has continually told me we are just friends. Could he have been hiding it just like I was?

Alec continues, "Keegan will remember you. Who, by the way, is asking to see you." I look to Jake and want to tell Alec to tell him I'm busy, but I'd hate to be in his position. I think of the difficulty of trying to pick up pieces of my life that I couldn't remember. I turn to Jake and give him a gentle kiss on his lips. "Jake, I'll be back. I love you, so please come back to me."

My brother walks me to the door of Keegan's room and I stop before I go in. "I can't do this." I turn to run away, but my brother doesn't let me.

"I'm going to go spend some time with Jake. You need to talk to Keegan. Even with all his screw-ups, he was a good friend to

The Broken Girl

you. I don't know how I feel about you being with him, after learning the truth while you were gone, but that doesn't mean I don't want you to make your own choice. I will not stop you from whoever that is, as long as they take care of you. I'm done trying to control your life and make sure it's perfect. Instead, I'm going to help you keep your secrets, if that's what you need, or I'll be the big brother who kicks some ass. Whatever it is. That's me now, okay, Becca?" I nod and hug him before turning around and walking through those doors to Keegan.

Seeing Keegan is the best and worst thing all at once. I see in his eyes that he doesn't remember me and our connection is gone, although I still feel this guilt to stick by him. Even after everything that's happened with Sarah. He needs me right now and, if he'll let me, I will help him through this. If he doesn't remember me, I could remember for the both of us, as a friend or as more. But I feel that it should be his choice. Until he's back on his feet and we see how this goes, I will play the amazingly supportive girlfriend even though I'm not sure if I want to be with him at all. I can't exactly dump my boyfriend when he needs me. What does that make me? So if I leave it up to him, I might not feel this guilt.

"Hello, Bec." Every time he says that name, it feels like it slices into my heart. He's never called me Bec and to hear it shows how much I don't mean to him anymore. Friend or otherwise.

"Becca. It's Becca." I say it sweetly but I see by his eyes that he's wondering if I'm upset with him.

"Sorry, I talked with your brother a bit and he did mention that. Must have forgotten." I have this innate urge to laugh. By the smirk on his face, he does too. So we both laugh.

It feels nice to laugh with him again, to move past our history. "So, I'm confused as to how we met and also about what happened with Sarah." Hearing her name brings back the night that Keegan and I had sex for my first and only time. Hearing him say goodnight to her led me to flee in the first place.

"I'm not sure what happened with Sarah. I'm assuming you and my brother lied to me. I came here in the spring and we met because you roomed together. I had a boyfriend, kind of, at the time." He nods his head to acknowledge me.

"Yes, Dillon, Alec told me everything that went down with him. He is one sick son of a bitch." I walk over and sit next to the bed in the chair.

The Broken Girl

"Was. He was one and yes, he was sick, mentally speaking. He just couldn't get the help he needed." I explain.

Keegan turns to me and I already know what he's going to ask. "Was?"

I haven't had to say it out loud yet but I know I can. "Yes, I killed him in self defense. He won't be hurting anyone else again. As for Sarah, I don't know. You will have to ask Alec." I change the subject because I just don't want to talk about Dillon anymore. "When I showed up for school we started to get close. You and my brother told me that Sarah was a summer fling. But since you don't remember the summer I guess that was a lie. I only found out it was more than that, after a fight when you slipped up and told me in a voicemail while you were half-drunk, right before our accident. But I started to move away and make my own friends because of the emotions involved with our friendship and because Sarah was still around. You couldn't let that happen or at least that's what you told me. Sarah caused problems and we let her. We got together and have had some issues, but we were trying to figure it out. Last thing you had said was that you loved me and we would fix this. I'm not holding you to any of this since you don't even know me to love me at all. I just need you to be okay, Keegan. Before we were together, we were very close friends. That, I will hold you to." I smile, hoping he gets what I'm saying and he gives me a small smile too.

"I'm a complete asshole, aren't I?"

I can't hold the laugh that falls out. "You could say that." I try not to, but I think of all the hurt I've went through when it came to Keegan; the comments about being a second fiddle to my dead boyfriend or my best friend, the angry and drunk comments. Of course, the thought unintentionally invades my mind about him saying goodnight to Sarah. I attempt to squash it. "But now, you get to be whoever you want to be. You are lucky you still remember your life."

"But I don't remember you." I shake my head, holding back the tears that are threatening to spill over my now glistening eyes.

"It could be worse and that's what we have to keep telling ourselves." Silently I kept saying that to myself, hoping I'll believe it, but right now all I can think of is how could this get any worse. "I will also be here for you to talk to and ask questions. If you want to know about us, then I can tell you. If you don't, then that's okay too. I

The Broken Girl

won't push anything on you. I was in an accident similar to this one before. I had pushed the memories out of my mind because they were too painful. Maybe you will remember one day, just like I did. If not, we will deal. I won't let you live every day waiting for the memories, Keegan, because you wouldn't have let me. You would have wanted me to move forward so that's exactly what you're going to do."

"That's something I do know about. You're talking about your accident with Michael. Your brother told me about that one night after we'd been rooming together for a while. I'm sorry that happened to you Bec… Becca." He gives me a small smile and I know he only remembers hearing my brother talking to him about me as Bec. I can't blame him, but it's a constant reminder of what we've lost. What we might never get back. I wasn't just talking about my accident with Michael. I was also talking about when Dillon had attacked me and left a butterfly. I remember him doing it and giving it to me, enough to give it to Jake before I was shipped off by ambulance. Although when I woke up, I had to be reminded. My heart hopes all he needs is a reminder, but I don't think this is going to be that easy. "Thank you, Keegan."

~ 20 ~

He looks flustered. I'm not sure what's causing it so I ask him, which only seems to make him even more flustered. "Guess you really do know me, eh?" I try to laugh but it comes out awkward. "Well Bec, I was wondering why you call me Keegan? Most people call me by my nickname Key or by my last name." Hearing him say that breaks my heart. I know he has no feelings for me because he is talking about this openly. My Keegan would have never asked me why I don't call him Key. Actually he insisted I didn't call him that.

"You never let me. You didn't even want me to know where it came from or what you had been like in the past." I can't help feeling like I'm looking at the past right now. He isn't the Keegan who had changed, he's the Keegan from the past. His nickname came from him having the ability to unlock any woman's panties. Hence, he was the Key to them. "Must have liked you if I didn't want you to know." I make a small gasp at those words, but he doesn't notice. *Liked?* Past tense and like is not enough... my Keegan loved me and now I know my Keegan is gone. Question is: will this Keegan love me and will I want to love this Keegan?

***

The Broken Girl

Being around Keegan is a challenge and being away from Jake is an even larger one. I spend my days with my brother and Keegan, staying on the sidelines listening to them. I go to my classes and do my homework while they talk about anything under the sun. I wrote my exams and did well considering the facts of my current life situation. The snow seems to be leaving and I'm looking forward to spring. Charlotte is adamant that we spend the summer away from all this, with no men in my life. A summer to myself, but I know I just can't do that. At least not until I know Jake is okay. As far as Keegan…well, he's okay, but I need to know he's *happy*.

"Becca, you can't stay in this room all day and only switch out to see Keegan. You only leave for school." I look up and see Alec looking at me from the doorway, I am sitting in the bed with Jake stroking his hair. He looks so pale. The doctors still aren't sure if he's going to pull through. When they say this, I usually just walk away. Jake *has* to make it. The alternative isn't an option.

"Becca, I'll give you five minutes and then you and I are leaving the hospital to go home. You will shower and eat something that's not from a vending machine or... I call Charlotte." I look at him, stunned because he knows Charlotte will drag me out of here kicking and screaming. It would make no difference to her. She's not embarrassed by anything.

"Fine. You win." He backs out of the room, giving me my time with Jake. "Jacob Kelso, you better be here when I get back and awake. I miss my best friend. You promised never to leave me, so I won't let you out of that one." Looking at Jake, even though he is pale and sick, he's still one of the most beautiful men I've ever seen. I wish more than anything he'd open those piercing hazel eyes and look at me. His honey brown hair is shaggier than it usually is and he has slimmed down a bit, but he is still solid. A hockey player through and through, no matter his ill state. I turn to snuggle into Jake. "I love you."

The door opens and I see my brother pop in. "Time's up."

Chapter Three

Keegan

I hear a knock at the door and I say come in. It's probably Alec or Bec.... His sister.... And my girlfriend. It's weird having a girlfriend I don't remember. Don't get me wrong; she's damn beautiful and I'm drawn to her but I still feel like something's not right. Like I don't deserve her.

"Hey, Key." I look up and see Sarah staring at me from the end of the bed and all those feelings come rushing back.

"Sarah..." She walks around to the side of the bed and sits on it with me. Her hand comes to my face and I lean in. As much as I know this is wrong I can't deny that I have feelings for Sarah. The Keegan that's with Bec might not have, but he's gone. "I'm so glad you're okay. I tried to come before but that friend of yours wouldn't let me in because of his sister."

Oh, yeah. Alec is going to be furious that she's here but I can't help it. I want to be near Sarah. "I'm glad you came. This is all so weird. Last thing I remember is us, being together, and everything being fine. What happened, Sarah?"

    I can see her eyes look down, trying to shield the tears that are begging to be released from the back of her eyes. "*She* happened." I'm taken back by this because I don't understand. If I felt the way about her that I still am feeling, then I don't see how that happened. "She came to visit her brother in the spring and after that you started to pull away. You started to come back during the summer. But as soon as she showed her face, we were different and you ended it. I get it. You were protecting her from that psycho ex of hers. But he's gone. I don't get why you're with her or stay with her. She was always with Jake. He slept in her room even when you were together. She hasn't been sleeping in her dorm or at Alec's while you've all been in the hospital. So if she's not sleeping in here with you, she's with him. She doesn't love you, Key, but I do. I love you." I look up and many things go through my head. If Bec and I were together then what the hell was she doing with my buddy Jake? I know they're friends but that seems to be beyond the friend zone. Why does hearing about Jake make me furious as shit too?

The Broken Girl

I sense Sarah lean towards me and I go the rest of the way to kiss her. I can't deny that it's still there. It's different from before but I still care about Sarah. I move my hand around her back and pull her tighter towards me as our kiss deepens. I feel her open her mouth slightly, allowing me access, and I take it. God, I miss this, but yet I feel odd. *Who cares? Clearly Bec's with Jake, right?* I put my hand under her shirt and she moans as my hand connects with her skin. It's an instant turn on and I'm getting more into this as it goes. I hear a squeak of the door followed by a gasp. We separate and I see Bec looking at me with her eyes wide and full of tears. It's like a ton of bricks have dropped on my heart. God, she wasn't kidding, I am an asshole.

Before I can say anything, she turns and runs out of the room with Alec just standing there, and not following her.

Sarah has a smug look. "Well, I guess she knows how we really feel about each other now, doesn't she? I'm going to go, but don't worry, I'll be back, Key. Love you." Sarah said with pleasure.

I turn to Alec and wish I could place the unfounded panic that has my heart racing at the fact that Bec just ran from the room. His eyes are on me and I feel like I deserve whatever he's about to do. "What did I just do?" I look to Alec, hoping to see my friend, but all I see is hurt in his eyes. Of course... it's his sister. Shit!

"Well if you were trying to hurt her, then I guess you did what you wanted to. Are you sure you don't remember the last year or so?" I'm speechless to what he's just said. Why would he think I'm lying about not remembering and why would this have anything to do with that.

"What do you mean, 'remember?' Of course not! Why in the hell would you say that shit?" He shakes his head and turns around so that I can't see his face. "You know what, Alec? Don't be pissed at me because, from what I hear, I'm not the only one stepping out of this relationship. You should ask your little sister Bec where she sleeps at night." Alec whips around and stalks up to me. I will admit that I pull back, wishing I'd played it cool. He's seriously pissed.

"Don't you dare! Don't ever put that shit on her, man! Jake is her best friend. Yes, she loves him but she loves you too. She was with you, Key. She never cheated on you. You're just letting that bitch Sarah screw with you like she always has when it comes to my sister. I won't let you, not this time, I'll push her to Jake and you will lose

The Broken Girl

the best thing that ever happened to you in your pathetic little life."

He takes a deep breath, letting out the anger. "But to answer your questions: you were together and, yes, when you weren't around she'd sleep with Jake. However, it wasn't sexual and you knew that. It was because of her nightmares from Dillon and the fear she had over it. He tried to kill her on a few occasions. Not to mention watching Michael, her boyfriend, die. So, pardon me that my sister's a little screwed up from all the shit that's happened to her. But what the hell is your excuse then?"

I'm furious she's been in Jake's bed and we were together.

"Well, Jake and her better not be doing that anymore." I see the anger return to his eyes but my anger won't allow me to calm down.

"Guess the Keegan we all know is still in there somewhere because of what just happened with Sarah. Well, that's exactly what he did when he was insecure about her loving him too."

"Time to pick, once and for all, Key. Is it Becca or is it Sarah? I sure as hell don't see what choice it really is, but with everything that's happened, I sympathize with you. I wouldn't know what to do, but man, you can't keep them both." I nod because I know he's right. I just wish I could remember everything so I could make the right choice. I guess that would just be too easy.

"She needs to make one too. She can't have both of us. I won't rush her because Jake's sick, but she has to make a choice."

He looks at me somberly and nods. "Don't I know it. Now get your head outta your ass and stop screwing around with this Sarah shit. If you want Becca, or even want the possibility of having Becca, then Sarah has to go. Sarah's had it out for Becca from day one. If you choose to see Sarah, that is your choice. I will understand. However, I can't have you living with me. Becca needs to feel safe and I'm going to talk her into moving back in with me."

"I think I'm in love with Sarah though. I just can't explain it."

Alec just shakes his head and looks at the floor. "Then I guess I will start packing your stuff. I'll talk to the dorms and see if we can get you in there for the rest of the semester."

I shake my head. "No, no dorms. I just want a small apartment of my own."

He nods and says he will bring me some ads. "I hope you don't ever remember, man. If you did, you'd hate the choice you just made." With that, he turns on his heels and walks out the room.

"I think I love Bec too, though." I know he didn't hear me but I said it anyways. I just wish I could remember her. What if I'm making the mistake he thinks I am? Or what if I choose her and I'm not remembering that even with Bec, I still loved Sarah. Either way, I'm screwed. Isn't that just great shit!

Chapter Four

Becca

Keegan and Sarah. I can't continue to compete with her. She wants Keegan and clearly he wants her. I won't stand in the way anymore. I will be his friend but I won't fight to keep what doesn't seem to be mine. First, he did stunts like this even before we got together. Then, during my first time, he says *her* name. *Come on, Becca! How much more do you need to realize it's over between you two.* I ran, I'd admit to it. I couldn't watch that, not again. I'm tired of fighting Sarah. But I will still be one of Keegan's best friends if he will have me, no matter the heartache it costs. Right now he needs friends that are going to be there for him and I won't turn my back on him. Not after everything he's done and given up for me. *Time to put on your big girl panties and be a friend. It's not like you even had made a choice as to who you love more. You are going to lose one of them.*

My inner thoughts have never been more right because as I push through the door to Jake's room, my body turns cold at

The Broken Girl

the sight in front of me. Doctor and nurses are rushing around the bed and Jake is hooked up to more wires and a breathing mask. I can't hear anything. The world is right there but yet so far away. I see them trying to stabilize him, but it's not working. *Don't leave me, Jakey.* I watched on, wishing my inner plea could reach him. I start to hear again and the world comes crashing in. I hear the beeping of his monitors slow and now the alarms are sounding. I hear someone say, "Call the OR." I feel like I'm going to pass out, I can't lose Jake. He can't die from trying to save me. I'm not worth that type of sacrifice. I see them push the button and the speakers are blaring, indicating a code blue in Jake's room. The next words make me sink against the wall, right to the floor. I sit there staring blankly, in a pile of scattered emotions.

"We're losing him!"

I'm still in a puddle on the floor when the door opens. Staring around the room, all around is disarray. Medical supplies are laying everywhere and the bed where Jake was is no longer there. "Becca, are you okay?" I look up to see Drake pulling me off the floor. I'm too shocked by what has happened to even understand the meaning of him being here.

I hear the door swing open again and shriek. "Becca!" Drake is holding me while Keegan yells at me, with my brother and Charlotte looking at me, stunned to our current surroundings.

"Where's Jake, Becca?"

I look to Alec, with no emotions left to convey. "He's been rushed to the operating room."

I don't move out of Drake's hold and Keegan's eyes are burning me. "What does that have to do with Drake being all over you?"

I hear Drake groan. He turns but doesn't let go of me. "I'm here because Charlotte asked me to come. We've become friends and I wanted to stop and see Jake before I went to find her. When I came in, I found Becca laying on the floor in shock and picked her up to comfort her." I pull tighter to Drake trying to hide from Keegan, since I haven't seen him since the Sarah incident.

"Let go of Bec. She's not yours Drake." Keegan is seething, but all I feel is the pain of being called Bec.

"She's not yours either, Keegan. From what the bitch new girlfriend of yours has being telling everyone, you and Becca are done." I peek out from Drake to see that Keegan doesn't deny it. *Why should he, Becca? He doesn't remember you.*

The Broken Girl

Keegan responds slowly, "I didn't. I don't know. I guess she's right." I turn my face away from his eyes because I just can't bear to look at him anymore.

"Key, don't act like you 'guess.' I asked you and you flat out said shit to cement that fact... Like I don't know you're moving out of our house?" Alec is furious; he has so much hate in his tone.

This is news to me and I tense. Drake pulls me closer and I'm in his full embrace as he strokes my back and hair. "How am I the bad one here? From what I'm told, she was like this, if not worse, with Jake. Why would I stick around for round two? Who knows, maybe this time it will be both Drake and Jake she's sleeping with at night."

I can't help the anger that comes over me and I blow up. I start screaming. "Get him out of here!"

I hear shuffling and then the door is shut. I look up to see just Charlotte left in the room. Drake is comforting me and I'm actually surprised that it doesn't feel off. I don't get the same vibe I did from him anymore. "Becca, let's go see if they have an update on Jake, okay?"

I look to Drake and see nothing but supportive eyes looking back at me. "Thank you, Drake." He turns and puts his arm around me, leading me to the nursing station, with Charlotte in tow.

"Alec will be back. He just took that good-for-nothing jackass back to his room." *God, I love Charlotte.* When a nurse comes to talk to us, we just listen. It feels like none of us are breathing. She told us that it's still too soon to tell, but that Jake had complications from his last surgery. He is in critical condition due to internal bleeding. She gives my hand a squeeze before leaving us in the waiting room closest to the operating room.

"Anything?" I see Alec and he has no emotions showing on his face. I know this face well. It means he's barely holding it together. I remember this same expression from when they told me Michael hadn't made it. "He's in critical condition, Potts. It's all we know." Drake looks at me and pulls me next to him. I lean into him. The next six hours are the longest of my life. At some point, I fall asleep with my head on Drake. When I awaken to hear the doctors coming through the door in search of us, I forget where I am momentarily. I find myself laying in Drake's lap with a blanket on me. "Are you the family of Jacob Kelso?"

We all nod and the doctors explain that it was touch and go for most of it. At one point they did lose him, but where able to

The Broken Girl

stabilize him and he seems to be doing well in recovery. They tell us that when he's moved to his room, it is fine for one of us to stay with him. "Who's Rebecca Potts?" I perk up and raise my hand. "His grandmother, who we called to notify, said that you're in charge of his care." Drake, Charlotte, and my brother just stare at me. I nod because this isn't exactly news to me.

"Will he be awake?" I finally find my voice, but it's still shaky.

"He's medicated now but we expect him to wake up in a few hours. We believe he will now make a full recovery." I feel like I breathe for the first time since I saw them take Jake away. "As soon as he comes through recovery, a nurse will be through to come get you." I nod and the doctors walk away.

"Becca, when did you become his next of kin?" Alec asks.

I look to Alec and I just shrug. "I didn't know until I got here and wanted to see him on the ICU floor. I guess when I was here and he wasn't allowed to see me, since it wasn't listed. After Dillon attacked me, he didn't want me to ever feel that helpless and not be able to be informed. That's what he told his grandmother and she wasn't fighting me on it. She said it's what he wanted."

~ 36 ~

Charlotte tries changing the subject. "Alec, I think we should leave and go get Becca something to change into and something to eat other than this hospital crap." Charlotte is trying to give me some space but I don't think I want to be alone. Drake's arm is draped over my shoulder and I don't feel alone with them all here.

"Charlotte, I don't want to leave Becca alone that long," Alec says.

I feel Drake tighten around me as he interrupts my brother. "I'll stay. Just bring me back something. Okay, Charlotte?" My brother looks at him with hesitation, but I nod to him giving him the okay. They pick up their jackets and hug me goodbye, leaving me sitting in the waiting room with Drake. What's even stranger is that I've never felt safe around him until now. *What has happened to my life?*

Chapter Five

Sitting and waiting to be allowed in to see Jake and being alone with Drake has become awkward. His arm is still around me, comforting me with his presence. It's completely friendly, which is so strange. However, he keeps opening his mouth to say something, and then he changes his mind. I see the inner thoughts stirring and I feel for him. He looks like he's trying to tell me the hardest thing in the world.

"Drake, thank you for staying with me, for finding me." He pulls his arm off me, causing me to flinch at the loss. He turns to look directly into my eyes. He grabs my face with each of his hands and pulls me closer to him. If anyone around us was watching they'd think he was going to kiss me, but I know that's not what this is. There is such sadness in his eyes that it's breaking my heart for the pain I know he must be feeling. "Don't ever thank me, Becca, not after how I treated you. Not after everything I've done. Please don't thank me." I see tears in his eyes and I pull him toward me, hugging him tightly. His head is on my shoulders and I feel the wetness from his tears now coming through my shirt.

I sit there for what seems like forever, just holding him, before he begins to talk. "Becca, I am so sorry for everything I've said to you. I just wish you could forgive me for being such an ass. I was going through a hard time when I came back to school. I should have waited longer before I came back. I never would have treated you that way if I had dealt with all my shit. Don't get me wrong, I'm a man and you are beautiful. I was hitting on you, but then I just hated you. None of that was your fault. I never meant to be this guy who you had to avoid. My...." The tears are falling down his face and I put my hand in his to show him that he's not alone. "My sister died right before I met you and I just... you reminded me of her. She never took shit from me or anyone else and that drew me to you. I was intrigued, but when I found out you were Alec's little sister, I hated you. I hate him because he still gets to have a little sister. Her death is my fault and I shouldn't get to have you in my life now either."

I shake my head at his words. "It's not your fault, Drake. I know better than most that sometimes bad things happen and it's

The Broken Girl

no one's fault." I look to his eyes and I see the hurt lying behind those crystal eyes.

"She took sleeping pills and never woke up. She killed herself, Becca." I do the only thing I can think of and embrace him with all the unspoken emotions I'm feeling at this point. "Jake came to me after what happened with you and Keegan. He told me that you took some extra pills. He asked me questions about you because of my history. After my sister died, I started working for a suicide hotline. When he told me what had happened, I just felt like the similarities where ripping me open. I hated you more than anything after that moment."

I remember the night that Jake had struggled to wake me. I just wanted to sleep without dreams and without being kept awake by my broken heart, after finding Keegan fooling around with Sarah. Jake was sure that I might have done it on purpose but I told him it was an accident. He must have gone to Drake after that. It also explains why Drake was going out of his way to make my life hell afterwards and couldn't look at me without a hateful look in his eyes. "I'm so sorry about your sister, Drake, but that doesn't make you a bad brother and it one hundred percent doesn't make you at fault. Take it from a little sister… sometimes

we do things that we may regret. We might
get into trouble, we might feel alone and sad,
just wanting this life to end. But her taking
her own life was not your fault. I'd never
want Alec to walk around with that guilt
weighing on his shoulders."

Drake has made so many things clearer
by his admission to me about our history. I
would never have guessed he had all this
bottled up inside. "Becca, you can't do that
to Alec. I know about everything and that it
wasn't only an attempt. Just remember that
no matter what happens, there are people
that love you. Even though I'll admit that
your life is pretty screwed up and it is in a
royal sort of way, but I've learned that it's
selfish. In my opinion, at least, I don't want
you to think that if you are upset or just need
a friend to talk to, that you're not alone. You
can talk to me. I'll be around, anyway. I…
well, I am kind of into Charlotte."

I look and Drake is blushing! I've never
seen him like this and when we were out as
a group, he always had a girl with him. He
always liked when girls were interested in
him. Except for Sarah, something about her
always seemed to piss him off. "I never
thought I'd see the day, Drake. Charlotte
hasn't said a word… which isn't a bad thing.
It means she probably likes you as much as
you like her."

The Broken Girl

I hear an odd noise and I see it's Drake. He's trying to suppress his laugh. "God, I hope so."

"Becca, this stuff with Keegan and Jake. Well, it's screwed up, that's for sure. But I still think you love them both. Probably in different ways and to have that connection taken away from you is so fucked up. Sarah is a bitch and she's seen her opportunity to swoop in. She's a tramp and always has been. Hopefully, Keegan will snap out of it and remember all that. If not and he doesn't see what's in front of him, it's his loss. No lack of memories should stop him from seeing what's right there. Jake too. They both need to wake up and smell the damn coffee that is Becca Potts. I've seen you with them and with Alec. Jake told me about Michael and I know it's hard to lose those you love. But you just keep kicking, even when the psycho ex was trying to knock you off. That right there should show them that you're amazing. No matter what, it's your choice. Don't just pick Jake because Keegan doesn't remember you. Don't pick one that's just a second choice. You deserve to be happy. No matter what, you need to come talk to me before you think of doing anything like take an extra pill to sleep. I'll stay all night with you. I won't let your brother live through my hell."

"Drake, I promise no matter how bad things get between all this drama, I would never take my own life. I didn't fight so hard against Dillon to just do it myself. No matter what happens with the guys, I'll be fine. I have my brother and Charlotte… and well, now I have a new friend who I can talk to." I nudge him and laugh, trying to lighten the mood. "Well, now it's my turn to say something. I never thought I'd see the day that Becca could have a man friend she wasn't secretly in love with. Unless there's something you want to tell me, Becca?" He gives me this mischievous look and busts out laughing at what I assume is a very serious look of hatred coming off my face.

"You're such as asshole, Drake." I push him away and can't hold it in anymore. I start laughing so hard that I feel tears coming.

"Don't you forget it Becca." For a minute, I forget everything. I forget the chaos that has come of my life.

I hear footsteps and a door swing open. I look to see a nurse coming towards us with a small unsure smile on her face. My heart stops beating and I haven't taken a breath when she speaks. "Mr. Kelso has been moved to his room on the surgical floor. I will be happy to show you up there, but unfortunately it's only immediate family or next of kin allowed, and only one."

I look to Drake and he nods at me to follow the nurse. "I'll move to the waiting area up there and message Charlotte so she knows where you are. I'm not going anywhere."

I give him a hug and kiss his cheek before turning to the nurse. "Thanks, Drake." He just nods. As I begin to walk away with the nurse, I asked the question I'm dying to know. "Has Jake woken up yet?" I feel all the air being sucked out of my body as her face falls and she answers me.

"No, honey. I'm sorry, but he hasn't."

Chapter Six

I now walk into the room where Jake lay unconscious. My heart literally stops. He barely looks like Jake. He has cords connected everywhere. Monitors beep at a steady pace, which I take to be a good thing. Seeing him there, pale and covered in bandages, makes me feel like my breath is escaping me "Oh, Jakey." I go to walk up to him, to touch him, but stop short and look to the nurse. "It's okay to touch him and you can be on the bed next to him. Just don't touch his incision areas or put any pressure on his abdomen. In a few hours guests will be allowed to visit him as per doctor's okay. The doctors will be by in the morning to talk to you about his medical status." I nod and wait for her to leave before climbing in the bed with him. I turn towards him and begin to sob softly, being careful not to put any weight on him. "Jake, you can't leave me too. Please stay with me. I'm nothing without you."

The Broken Girl

I must have dozed off because I hear noises and open my eyes to see Alec, Drake, and Charlotte looking at me, talking quietly. "How long was I out for?" Looking over to Jake, he is still the same, no change to his body placement or anything. I feel my heart sinking. *God, Jake, wake up! I need you.*

"They let us in about half an hour ago. You must have fallen asleep just after coming in here. You look exhausted, Becca. I think I should take you home."

I shake my head and yell. "No, Alec, I won't! He didn't do it to me when I was lying here. I won't do it to him. Stop asking me! It's not helping me, for God's sake! Just stop it!" I immediately regret my response when I see my brother flinch. Drake walks up to me and grabs me off the bed and brings me into the chair, and onto his lap. I look to see Charlotte closely watching, but not in a jealous way. But in awe of Drake's ability to comfort me and my willingness to let him.

"Potts she didn't mean it." I nod in agreement, looking towards Alec, and hoping he understands.

"Becca, I'm sorry. I just hate seeing you like this." Charlotte grabs my brother's hand and pulls him into a hug.

"Why don't we go get some coffee for everyone. The doctors will be in soon." It was morning already. I guess the nurse didn't let them in until later than she had anticipated.

I stay in Drake's arms, trying to wrap my mind around everything that's going on. I've lost Keegan and I'm losing Jake. The door opens and I look, expecting Charlotte and Alec to have returned, but it's the doctor. I try to straighten up but I'm just so exhausted. Drake helps me sit up, but I'm still in his lap. "Miss Potts, I'm Dr. McNeil. I was the one that operated on Mr. Kelso. We feel that the surgery was successful, however, he should have woken up already. It's not unheard of for it to take this long, but due to the fact that he never regained consciousness from the attack previously, it's hard to tell or give a time line." He continues talking but I'm not hearing anything anymore and they eventually just talk to Drake. When they've said all they came to say, they leave and I turn to Drake, weeping.

"Drake, why won't he wake up?" I fall into full hysterical sobs, unable to catch my breath.

"I don't know, Becca. He's just taking his time." I shake my head against Drake's chest.

The Broken Girl

"I need him." I feel Drake's hand in my hair, brushing it down. I feel like somehow I've gained not just a friend but also a brother.

"You are not the type of girl you leave if you can help it, Becca. He knows what's waiting for him he will wake up."

We sit like this in silence until my brother and Charlotte return with food. "Alec, I'm so sorry. I just… I'm sorry. I didn't mean to snap on you like that. It was unfair of me to do that. You are hurting just as bad as I am." He walks over and takes me away from Drake, and envelops me in a big hug. I notice that Charlotte has now taken my place with Drake and, for a minute, I forget what's going on around me. I look at them and wonder how all this happened. Charlotte has never been one to fall into it with the bad boy, but I guess Drake really isn't that person. He's just as broken as I am. She looks generally happy with him and that's something I've never seen Charlotte experience. When Alec lets go of me he takes his seat and pats beside him. I shake my head in response, walking over to the bed to sit with Jake.

We are all talking about stories involving Jake, figuring we could embarrass him out of his slumber. "Did I ever tell you when I yelled for him at the door to come kill the spider in my room?" Everyone looks at me and is laughing before I even realize this is going to be good. They all shake their heads, indicating I hadn't told them of this before. "Well, Jake came busting through the front door of my dorm, looking all bad ass like he was going to do some serious ass kicking. When he asked me what was wrong, I was cowering on my bed with my pillow and just pointed up at the ceiling above him. He looked up and laughed at me for being scared of a spider. That was until the silly thing dropped from the ceiling and he screamed like a little girl. But not before running and jumping on my bed and hiding behind me for his own safety from the big bad spider." We are all laughing hysterically when the door opens and my mouth drops open as to who's standing there staring at us.

"Well, hello, Becca. I've just come to stop in and see Jake before going to see Keegan, *my boyfriend*." She drags out the last words and makes me cringe in anger.

"What, you don't have enough to keep yourself busy, Sarah?" My brother gives her a dirty look that makes me wonder what he's talking about.

"I never have too much going on to prevent me from making this one's life a little darker."

The Broken Girl

Charlotte shoots up from Drake's lap and goes right in front of Sarah. "You better get your skanky bitch ass out of this room, before I let my cousin drag you out again by your hair like she did before." I see my cousin smirk and so does Alec, who had witnessed my little takedown with Sarah this past school year.

"Jake doesn't even like you, Sarah. Just get out of here and stop wasting your time. Go see Keegan and help him remember his last several months. Oh, wait, you can't because he knew you were a slut and broke up with you for me." She takes a step forward but Charlotte puts her hand up to stop her. Before Charlotte can tell her off, Drake beats her to it.

"We all know the only reason you have Keegan now, Sarah, is because he can't remember Becca. Don't think you've won. Because if he remembered everything he had with Becca, he wouldn't touch you with a ten foot pole. Jake won't go near you, so give it up." She looks like her head is about to spin around and have steam start coming out of her ears.

"We will see about that." With that, she spins and rushes out the room off to see her precious Keegan, I'm sure. That knowledge

~ 50 ~

makes me nauseous until I hear something that lifts my heart and soul.

"Thank god, the wicked bitch of the west is gone." I almost don't want to turn to the side in case I'm dreaming. It came out raspy, but even so my heart melts at hearing his voice.

"Jake, thank god." I turn and hug him, causing him to wince slightly. "I'm sorry… for everything." I have tears coming down my cheeks and he brushes them away.

"And you should be sorry." I blanch at this and wait for him to tell me he hates me for all this trouble. For dragging him into this and almost killing him. "You promised you'd never tell anyone about that damn spider, Becca."

Chapter Seven

Trying not to blink just in case my eyes open again to find him still in a coma, I just stare at Jake. "Becca." I hear shuffling and a door closing from behind me. I turn and see that they've left me alone with Jake. When I look into his eyes and see that he's staring at me with worry, I break into tears. He goes to put his arm on me and I push myself off the bed and move to the corner of the room. "What are you doing? I can't touch you if you're over there." I shake my head profusely because I know I don't deserve this. "I don't deserve the comfort of your touch, Jake. I don't deserve to be standing in this same room with you."

I hear the blankets move and Jake tries to sit up. He quickly gives up. "Becca, come here." I shake my head at him. "Jake, I'm the reason you are in that bed. I'm the reason you almost died." Jake just stares at me before he answers. "Becca, I love you. Stop this and come over here." I back away towards the door and I see panic go across his face. His expression quickly changes to anger. I turn around and grab the door handle to reach my escape. "GOD, Becca! Why can't you just let someone love you..." Jake never yells at me and this brings back the tears.

"Because that got someone killed the last time. Then I fell in love again and it nearly killed people. My love is toxic, Jake. I'm toxic! Don't you see that?" I'm barely able to catch my breath as I say the words that have been plaguing me for far too long. "My love kills people, Jake. You'd all be better off without me in your lives. I've been thinking and I'm leaving, Jake. When this semester is done, I'm leaving, and I don't think I'm coming back."

"Rebecca Potts, get your twiggy ass over here right now!" I keep my eyes on the floor, hoping he'll just let me walk away. I feel like all I do is cause them to be put in jeopardy. "Move it, Rebecca, or so help me, God, I will get out of this bed and pop all these stitches to get to you." I sulk and start walking over to the side of his bed, but I don't look at him. His hand tucks under my chin and pulls my eyes to him. I try and blink back the tears. I see that he has unshed tears in his eyes, causing what little power I'd had to control my emotions to fade. I begin to sob, standing next to the bed with

The Broken Girl

Jake. I feel his hand leave my face. He grabs my arm and pulls me into the bed beside him. I feel guilty immediately for the comfort I'm feeling. "Jake, please let me leave. I just bring more trouble."

"Becca, what in the hell are you talking about?" I hadn't told anyone about the note that was left under my door that I found this morning. I feel its presence in my pocket, causing this heavy burning feeling. I can't tell him or he will worry. No one can know. I have to keep this from everyone. "Jake, you are hurting because of me. I love you and that almost got you killed. I won't… I can't… please, don't make this harder than it already is." I try to pull away but he won't let go.

"I go where you go, Becca, and don't forget that. Whatever happened with Dillon, I would not let it change us. Keegan won't either. Neither of us will blame you for this. It wasn't your fault. We both love you." I jump out of the bed and push against the wall before Jake realizes I'm gone. "Becca, what?" I shake my head because I realize that no one has told Jake about Keegan. I slide down the wall and just keep rocking back and forth, unable to tell him the words I haven't said it out loud. Saying it to Jake will make it real and I'm not sure I'm ready for that.

"ALEC!!" I vaguely hear Jake yelling, but I can't come out of this. When he finds out the damage has been permanent for Keegan, he will hate me for this. Jake will get better but there is no guarantee that Keegan will ever get that year and a half back. I feel myself being picked up but I know it's not by Alec. It is Drake. "Breathe, Becca. Just take deep breaths." I feel my chest tightening and my breath becoming uneven. I'm having an anxiety attack; I open my eyes and see Jake staring helplessly from his bed. His eyes tell the confusion and they narrow when Drake puts me on his lap in the chair beside the bed. "Drake, what are you doing? What's going on? Becca hates you? Why did she freak out about Keegan? What the hell happened while I was…"

I turn in Drake's lap and look at him. "Do you want me to tell him, Becca?" I shake my head at Drake, but my heart melts at his kindness.

"I don't hate Drake. We came to an understanding and got everything on the table. He's also with Charlotte." The tightness of Jake's face turns to one of realization that there is nothing going on between Drake and I. *Like I need another guy in my life right now to cause more chaos.*

The Broken Girl

    I climb off of Drake's lap and he gets up to follow me. "Are you okay?" I nod, knowing he is going to leave me to do this on my own. "I'll be right outside if you need me, Becca." He gives me a hug and a kiss on the top of my head, just like Alec would. Once he walks out, I turn to Jake and he's almost angry looking. "So I must have missed something. Since when would you let Drake do that? You sure he's with Charlotte?"

    I figure out why Jake's angry and it surprises me. "What? Jake, are you jealous? There is nothing going on with Drake, God! The only reason we are this way is because of his sister and what you told him about me. He thought with everything going on that I may need a friend." Jake's eyes narrow on me again and I step back. It felt like he had pushed me with his eyes.

    "You are with Keegan anyways."

    I look to the floor because I didn't want to have this conversation. "No, I'm not, actually." Peeking up, I see that Jake's hand is outstretched to me and I grab it.

    "What happened, Becca?"

    Taking a deep breath before continuing, I'm hoping my voice doesn't fail me now. "After the accident, you were unconscious, but so was Keegan. When he woke up… he

~ 56 ~

didn't remember the last year and a half or… me. Last he remembers, he was with Sarah. So that's who he is with now."

I feel Jake push my hand away and I feel like I've been slapped. "That's why you are not together then, right?"

I'm in the bed with him before he can even process what I've done. "God, Jake, No. Don't you see, Jake? It's you. When everything went bad, I ran to you. Doesn't that show anything?" He tries to push me away and I let him.

"You're here with me because he doesn't remember you. If he did, you'd be with him right now and I'd be in here alone." I turn and put my fist into the wall that is now in front of me. I hear Jake gasp and I've even shocked myself at my action. Drake comes rushing in the room and turns to try and understand what's going on.

"Get her out of here, Drake. She's only here because Key doesn't remember her."

At this, I walk over to the door, but Drake grabs me before I make it out. "Jake, you are wrong, man. It's you. It always was you. Take it from me. I watched it happened. You two dumbasses may not have seen it but I did. Even Alec and Charlotte did. Stop the bullshit, Jake! This girl hasn't slept in her own bed since the accident." I see Jake's eyes dart to mine with a confused look.

The Broken Girl

"He's right, Jake. It's you. I just…" I can't find my words and I just stop talking.

"Jake, you're going to listen to what Becca has to say and you're going to believe her. This girl loves you, man, and more than she should with all the dumb shit you've done." Drake turns and walks out, giving us privacy again.

"If you had to choose between him and myself before all this shit changed and all this craziness happened, who would it have been?" Jake is looking at me and I wish I had some answers for him.

"I can only tell you what I was coming home to tell you, but things have changed, Jake. I can't give up on Keegan either. I love him, but… I love you more. You're the reason I ran. When I saw you with Kristy, I couldn't deal with it. I'd just done what I had with Keegan and I just… It was wrong. It shouldn't have been Keegan, but we had all this history with Dillon and you kept telling me you weren't in love with me. You kept pushing me to Keegan. I know you are not in love with me, Jake, but… Well, I am undoubtedly in love with you."

"And Keegan, how do you feel about Keegan?" I sigh because he's skirted over the fact that I love him. It pains me because

I know he doesn't love me back the same way.

"I love Keegan and you know that, but I was coming home to end things with him. It wasn't the right time for us."

Jake looks at me with questioning eyes. "Whose time is it then, Becca?" Jake is not able to look me in the eyes and I feel the sting of rejection.

"No one's, my love is broken. I'm broken. But I can't leave Keegan behind either. I will be his best friend; I will help him find his place. But his place isn't with me. No one's is." I see the hurt cross Jake's face and I realize my mistake right away. "Jake, I mean romantically. You're my best friend and that's never going to change."

"What if I want that to change?" I feel like I've been hit by a car and I can't catch my breath.

"Jacob, please don't say that. I need my best friend. I need you. I can't lose you too. Please don't leave me alone. I'm sorry. This entire thing is my fault and I know I shouldn't have you in my life after the danger I put you in. If I were smart, I'd leave now because I'm still putting you in danger. I feel like if I walked away now, my heart would always be here… here with you. I know you don't feel that way and that's fine, but I can't lose my best friend. Jake,

The Broken Girl

please don't do this to me." I look up to see him smirking at me. "Becca, come here."

I make myself walk the short distance to him and he grabs my hand, pulling me to sit beside him. I look down, unable to keep eye contact with him. He undoubtedly is about to break what little piece is left of my heart by telling me he doesn't want to be my friend. I feel his hands go on either side of my face and he pulls me down towards him. He lightly kisses my lips and I feel at first like it's a goodbye. Then suddenly it gets more heated as he presses his lips with more force and I let myself go. I bring my hand into his hair and kiss him with everything I have. Trying to put every ounce of love I have for him into it because this is all I'm ever going to get with Jake. "Becca." He whispers my name against my lips and I pull back, feeling the sting of rejection coming.

"Jesus, Becca. Just relax, okay? You're going to give yourself a heart attack." I go to slide off the bed but he grabs my hand.

"Goodbye, Jake." He doesn't let go of my hand and I turn to look at him with tears in my eyes, streaming down my face.

"Becca, are you really that dumb. I've loved you since I saw you by the lake when you visited Alec. You drew me in hook line and sinker at that very moment. I told you all those times that I wasn't in love with you because I thought it's what you wanted to hear. I'd rather have you in my life as my friend than nothing at all. I'd still rather have that, even if it were not what you wanted. I know right now that you are lost and I'm lost too, Becca. We need to heal, but when we've healed, I want to be with you. I want you to choose me and have no doubt that you want it to be only me." I nod. *Jake loves me? Maybe I am that dumb since I didn't see it.*

"We will get Keegan better, you will deal with all this, and I will get to leave the hospital. You will not feel guilty, Becca. I won't let you. Keegan wouldn't want you to and I don't want you to. I know we'd both do it again and get in that car to protect you, even knowing that this is going to be the outcome. I'd die for you, Becca. If I remember correctly, you didn't care much about your safety that night, only ours. So is it so crazy that we'd feel the same way?" Clearing all this with Jake makes things easier. "I only slept with Kristy because I heard Keegan talking about what his plans were for the night. I wanted to punch him and go all cavemen, dragging you out of there. I'm sorry, Becca. Wait... where did you sleep this whole time?"

The Broken Girl

"Really, Jake, you have to ask? I was here with my bed buddy every night the doctors would allow me to be, which was every night, except when you were in recovery. Don't you see, Jake? It's you. I love you, Jacob Kelso, always have, and always will. This isn't going to be an easy road, but I'll do whatever I have to do to be with you and deal with everything head on. I know if I can get out from under my past, we can maybe make this work and be together." I feel his hand squeeze mine.

"Not maybe. We *will* work this out, Becca." For a minute, I let my heart feel his words. The weight of the note in my pocket soon brings the reality that I'm not safe to be around crashing back down.

"No, wait… Jake, no… I can't, it's not safe. Being around me is asking for trouble. Look at my track record. One dead boyfriend and one with no memory. I won't put you in danger too." Jake is watching me as if he's trying to figure out what's going on.

"Dangerous? No, Becca. What are you talking about?" By instinct, I put my hand over my pocket to protect it and to protect him from it. "Becca, what's in your pocket?" *If anyone should see this, it's Jake. Maybe it will make him see how dangerous I really am to be around and he will let me go, because that's the only way I'm getting out of this room.* I reach in and pull out the note, placing it in Jake's hand.

"He may not have finished the job, but I will."

Chapter Eight

"Becca, what the hell is this?"

"I don't know, Jake. I found it under my dorm room door."

Jake looks at me and I can see he's skeptical. "And is this the only one you've gotten?"

I try and put on my big girl face to show I'm not scared but I know I've already played my cards by telling him I'm dangerous to be around. "Jake, it's probably just someone trying to screw with me." I already can see that he isn't buying my brave act.

"Becca, I hope you are right, but if you are not, I will always save you." I slip onto the bed beside him, bringing my hand to his face. When my hand makes contact with his cheek, he leans in. I feel the warmth that has returned to his body rub against my skin.

"But who will save you, Jake? I'm not going to let you get hurt again."

"As long as you're safe then I am saved, Becca."

***

The last three days that I've spent with Jake, I've seen Sarah in the halls going to see Keegan but I haven't gone to see him. Sarah hasn't come to see Jake again. It's probably because now that he's awake, he'd tell her to get out. Drake and Charlotte have been attached at the hip and have been here every night. Alec hasn't really said much to me, but he is continuously staring at me all the time. I feel like he wants to say something but doesn't. He has been spending a lot of time with Keegan and I think that guilt is bothering him because he feels torn. Jake is getting to go home in a few more days and he is adamant that he goes where I do. My brother hasn't asked where I'm going but I can't live with Keegan and see him falling into Sarah's games.

"Becca, can I talk to you?" I turn from Jake, looking to Alec with a puzzled look. I look to Jake silently asking if he told my brother about the note but he just shakes his head.

"I don't think this is the right time, Alec?" Drake seems to know that whatever is about to happen, I'm not going to like. I can't just not talk to my brother. "Sure, I'll

The Broken Girl

be right back." With that, I turn from Jake. As I walk, his hand slides out of my fingers and I hate the lack of our touch. Once we get out into the hall I expect him to talk to me, but he just puts his arm around me and leads me further away from Jake's room.

"Becca, I know you don't want to hear this but we have to talk. It's about Keegan. I've asked him to move out..." My heart plummets and I take a step back. *Keegan has lost so much and now he's losing his home although it's not like he remembers the house.* "And, well, he's agreed." The sting still hurts from knowing I won't see Keegan around anymore. "I'd like you to consider living with me, but if you don't want to, that's fine. But your room will still be there for you. Keegan is moving into his own place in the apartments across the street from our house, and not with Sarah." I can tell he's added the last part for my benefit but it doesn't lessen the blow.

"Keegan's is being released today." I don't look at my brother but continue to look out the window. I've now found out that it gives me an escape from all this. "Becca..." I knew he was going to be released. I just hoped he'd get his memory back first. "Becca... He's asking to see you."

Hearing that, my eyes snap from the window to my brother's face. I can tell immediately that he's not asking because he remembers me. "I don't think I can do that, Alec, Why does it matter anyway? It's not like he knows me. He just has some misplaced guilt about everything that's happened. He feels he needs to see me and say words I don't want to hear. Just tell him that it's fine and I'm fine. Everything is fine, okay?"

I hear my brother make a sound that almost comes off like a growl and I see that he's furious to my response to him. *Oops!* "REBECCA POTTS, you are going in there and you're going to let him say what he needs to. That's Keegan in there not some nobody! He has been there for you and you damn well are going to be there for him in whatever capacity he needs. He... God, Becca, he needs you even if he can't remember. I know I have no right to ask this of you or to involve myself, but I can't help it. I need you to wait. Don't move on with Jake yet. Please, just give Keegan more time. If he wakes up from all this and realizes that he's lost you, I don't know what will happen."

"He loves you and I know you love him. I know you love Jake too, so just wait. I know Jake will wait because, just like

The Broken Girl

Keegan would, he wants you to make the best decision for yourself. They both want you to be happy and they are both willing to settle with just being friends to have you in their lives. Just be Keegan's friend, that's what he needs right now." I shake my head, feeling the weight of tears in my eyes.

"He doesn't need my friendship. He doesn't remember me." I feel my brother's fingers swipe away the tears that have now started to fall down my cheeks.

"Becca, he might not remember you, but he feels the loss of your presence. It's time to show him that what he feels he's missing isn't gone. It is just broken and it can be repaired, I promise."

"You should be able to wait and let things happen naturally. Don't rush into things with Jake. I will support whatever makes you happy. But remember that if you go there with Jake, you risk losing your friendship. So make sure when you make a choice that you are making the right and final one." I feel like my brother has shamed me and I want to hate him for getting involved, but I can't. Keegan is his best friend and I wouldn't expect any less from him. He's not wrong. I do love Keegan, but I love Jake too. It's always been Jake I ran too. But... does that mean that it's more love than the feelings I have for Keegan? "If you really love Keegan, you should be able to remember that love for the both of you, Becca." My eyes are wandering around, looking for any escape from these overwhelming emotions.

"Because if you were in Keegan's spot, he'd never give up on his love for you."

The Broken Girl

Chapter Nine

Keegan

When I asked Alec to see his sister, I see hope in his eyes. At least until I say that I just want to talk to Bec alone. For someone reason, I just can't adjust to calling her Becca. I knew her as Bec, so that's just how it's stayed in my head. "Sure, man." I know he doesn't want to bring her to me. He'd probably rather punch me in the head. *Hey, there's a thought. Maybe it will bring back my memory.* When he left, I felt my chest tighten, with what feels like fear, about what she's going to say to me. *What the hell is wrong with my dumb ass? I've never felt shit like this before, not even with Sarah.* That scares the shit out of me even more because I wish I could remember her. And why do I feel this constant panic without her around? I get up to put all my stuff in the corner, and wait. "Hey, dude, I just wanted to find out when you want me to take you to your place."

Drake hasn't said much, but to give the man credit, I haven't been up to much talking.

"I'll be ready soon... I'm waiting to talk to Bec." I see Drake tense and I'm surprised as shit by his reaction.

"BECCA. Her name is Becca." I don't need to justify my shit to him.

"Always be Bec to me and I don't think she needs another dick trying to get to her, eh, man?" Before I can regret what I've said I am pushed up against the wall of my hospital room.

"Becca will always be Becca. Just cause your brain is having a shit time doesn't mean you will treat her like an option, man. I won't let it and if Potts heard that shit you just spewed out of that dumbass mouth of yours, you'd be sporting a fat lip. I don't think it's a good idea, man. Just let her go with some of her heart left intact, man."

I move out of his grasp and try to comprehend his words. "What if I can't let her go though?"

"Ah, Key, I can't tell you what to do, man, but this whole thing is just messed up. Becca is barely keeping it together; Jake is doing well and will be heading home soon. Before you get your shit out of joint, they aren't together because, unlike that tramp you are fucking with, Becca doesn't move on like a hooker looking for her next fix. So

The Broken Girl

remember that shit when you wake up and have put her through hell with all this Sarah shit. If you break her, I will break you, and don't doubt that. Text me when you're done and you better leave her in the same condition or better than what she came to you in." With that, he stomps out, leaving me reeling from his rant.

I'm still trying to get my shit together when I hear a soft knock at the door and Bec peeks her timid face in. "Can I come in, Keegan?" She's beautiful, and not just in an 'I want her way.' She's so beautiful, it should be damn well illegal. Wars would be fought over this beauty. *I'd fight till my death for her.* Whoa! Where in the ever loving hell did that come from?

"Thanks for coming, Bec. I wanted to talk to you, if that is alright?" She nods and all I see is this gorgeous creature looking at me. Her eyes are the bluest eyes I've ever seen; the only way to describe them is that they are crystal blue. You can see so much of what she is feeling by her eyes and she wants to be anywhere but here with me. I feel a pain in my heart as I realize I've caused her this feeling. She has this long blonde hair that has different shades in it now that she's fully under the light. Her body... Well, I know what I want to do to it and it's nothing I'm ashamed of. Shit, how could I have not gone there with her? If I did, how come I can't remember? In this florescent light, no one is supposed to look this damn beautiful. She goes to open her mouth to talk but all I see are her lips, pink and perfect, just like the rest of her. *I have to kiss her.*

"Keegan?" *Ah, shit, she was saying something and I was too busy looking at her lips to actually listen.* "You wanted to see me?" I don't know what I've done to her to make her this way. I have this feeling that I should be the only one feeling timid and embarrassed, as if I've harmed her in some way.

"Yeah, Bec, let's sit and talk. Is that going to be alright?" She nods and I walk over to the bed and pat the bottom of it for her to come sit beside me. She follows, but is hesitant. She sits, but doesn't look me in the eyes and I want to reach out to her and I fear her damn rejection. Against my better judgment, I bring my hand up and lay it on top of hers. I feel her eyes linger on the spot where my hand is, but I can barely keep my breath in check. Touching her damn well knocked the wind out of me.

"Keegan, are you okay?" she finally asks.

The Broken Girl

Great. I probably look like a damn stalker with how I'm staring at her. Get your shit together, Key! "Yup, I'm fine. I wanted to talk to you about everything… I just…" She interrupts me and I want to be mad, but the sound of her voice makes everything else go away. At least until I actually hear the words coming out of her mouth and then I begin to panic.

"Keegan, it's fine. You're with Sarah or something. I understand you don't remember me; we can still be friends, of course. That is, if you still want to be my friend." I don't know what's going on but my heart and body aren't listening to my head.

I grab her by the sides of her face and crash my lips against her. She tastes so damn sweet. God, she's perfect. I hear her moan lightly against my lips and I swear that's the sexiest sound I've ever heard. I crave it and want more of it. I take my chance and deepen the kiss, tracing my tongue along her bottom lip until she gives me access to her mouth. I dive in and claim what's mine. *What the hell? What's mine?* I feel her start to pull away, but I don't let her. I slip my arm around her back trying to give her everything I've got so that all this messed up shit doesn't mean that I don't get to see her again.

"Keegan…"

I feel her hands on my chest and I pull away. Her lips are shining and I want to immediately dive back in. *Damn, this girl is addictive.*

Deep down, I know all this shit is going to come crashing down. Shit never goes right with me and I will end up screwing it all up. I have a feeling I've done something before the accident to already make me lose this beauty that's sitting here, not even understanding how goddamn beautiful she is. "God, I wish I could remember you." I see a tear coming down her cheek and I wipe it away. "I wish I could give you what you want and it's killing me that I can't." No truer words have ever been spoken. I want her. I want everything with her but I just know I won't get it.

"Me too. Keegan. Me too."

I can't be who she wants and needs. I'm not that guy. I might have been before the accident, but whatever changed me to deserve this girl isn't around anymore. I'm not that guy. I wish I were because it's hard not to love her even though I don't remember her. "Please don't leave and stay away from me. I need you and I want to remember, but if it doesn't happen. I still

The Broken Girl

want to have you in my life anyways. I think it's important. Please tell me you will stay." *I'm such a selfish prick.*

"Keegan, I will always be in your life." I feel my heart pick up but just like that, it comes crashing down again. She utters the words I dread hearing. "I'll always be your friend."

We talked about a few things, like me moving. She said she'd help and pack up what stuff is still left there and what is in her room of mine. I really want to ask her to let me go to her room, but that will lead to no good and is not fair to her. I can't give her everything she wants, no matter how much I want to. I can tell this space between us is killing her like it is me. She's going to leave. I can feel it before she even says it.

"I have to get back, but I will call you, okay? My number is in your phone if you need anything, Keegan. Just call me."

I nod and as she steps to the door, I feel the panic. I then ask the one thing I'm dying to know. "Bec, wait!" She turns and I see that it hurts to hear me call her that too but I just can't manage to call her Becca. It doesn't feel right. "What did I do? I did something to you before the accident?"

She shakes her head and goes to leave. "It's not important anymore, Keegan." I get up and grab her hand, pulling her back from the door.

"Please just tell me…how am I supposed to deal with all this if I don't know?" She looks so damn torn. I feel bad for this because it's obviously hurting her to rehash these memories.

"You called me Sarah." I drop my hand from hers and my whole body goes numb. *Okay, I get it, not cool but not the ending of the world unless?*

"Oh, I said it…" She nods and pulls away to the door but I don't stop her this time. She didn't deserve that. I don't know why I'd even think of Sarah if I had her touching me.

"You said it after. You were drunk, but it was my first time, and my only time. Goodbye, Keegan."

This girl was a virgin and I took that from her and called her my ex's name. Now I can't even remember her. She walked in on me with that same ex. *What a Jackass.* I'm so stunned that I don't even get to say bye. I just watch her walk out and leave me behind. *You just lost the best thing you've ever had.* One thing is for certain. I'm an asshole and I don't deserve her but that doesn't means I will let her go.

I'm a real selfish bastard.

Chapter Ten

Becca

What was that, Becca? I never expected it to be that way when I went in to see Keegan. The look in his eyes…he is so lost and so unlike the Keegan I know. I didn't see the Keegan I'd known in that room. Who I did see made my heart tighten in a way I rarely had happen with him before. I walk down the hall to the little visiting area they have. It's like a sunroom with some plants and a fish tank. It's the closest I can get to nature and I'm craving it. I don't hear anyone come in, so when I hear a voice say my name, I'm startled.

"Becca…" I turn to see Drake staring at me. "I'm just getting ready to take Keegan home, but I wanted to stop in and see if you needed anything. I know this has got to be hard on you, Becca. Everything that you went through with Michael was worse and now this. But you got through that and you can get through this."

"At least Michael died. I didn't have to watch him walk around with just me having the memories of us. Only the memories are dead. Keegan is here, thank God, but it seemed easier because I didn't have to see Michael not know who I was. Not remember that he loved me. Michael was just gone… Keegan, well I have to watch him be with someone else. To him, he knows nothing else; to me, it seems like in a blink of an eye I lost him. The difference is he's still here plaguing me and reminding of everything I've lost. It was easier with Michael… God, Drake, what's wrong with me that I feel this way?" I can't look at him; I can't believe I just said all that. Worse part is I meant and felt every word of it.

"Becca, he's just as lost as you are. He might not remember you, but he knows something is missing. If he didn't, he wouldn't have just begged my ass to bring you around when the team and everyone gets together."

I bring my hand up to my lips, which not long ago had Keegan's lips pressed against them. "I'm going to take him home. I will be back… but um… Jake is asking where you are." I begin to panic that Jake will know something is wrong or that I'm still feeling love for Keegan.

The Broken Girl

"Becca… I saw that he kissed you. It doesn't make you weak or a bad person for it. Just don't lie about it. Get in front of it. You are allowed to be confused." He gives me a tight hug, kissing the top of my head and leaving me here in the sunroom. The tears I'd been holding in since walking into that room with Keegan begin to pour out.

How much more can I take? I wish I knew because then I'd at least see an end to my pain. I hope Keegan remembers, not so that we can be together, because I really don't know how I feel anymore. But even if he never remembers me, this new guy he seems to be grabbed a bit of my heart too.

I wait twenty minutes before I go back to Jake's room, hoping he will not be able to tell I've been crying. "Becca, I thought you left." I shake my head, unsure if I trust myself to talk. "Becca, what happened? You were with Keegan, weren't you? Drake said he's getting to go home today."

Home? That's not his home. "What I'm about to say… Jake, you have to respond to this as my friend and if you can't, it just proves that we can't just be friends." I feel him tense, but he says nothing. "Keegan kissed me." I hear him gasp but don't look at him. Instead, I'm staring at the floral picture that is hanging from the wall in Jake's hospital room.

"Becca... look at me, okay?" I reluctantly pull my eyes from the picture to Jake's eyes. I expect to see anger or sadness but I'm met with his understanding eyes.

"I know this is hard, not just for you, but for Keegan. This whole thing is fucked up and there's no way around it. We just have to be honest so that we all make it through this in one piece. I know that none of what you are feeling means that you don't love me, Becca." I nod because I don't think I could open my mouth without sobs escaping. Jake knows me so well. How will I ever make this unbelievable choice? "We haven't really talked about this, but... I heard you, Becca. That night you said you loved me and that you were in love with me. That you didn't want me to leave you alone and that you needed me. Dammit, Becca, don't you see? I loved you before you even said one word to me. I saw this lonely girl sitting there at the lake, lost and alone, but I saw something in her. Hope, a new beginning, one that I wanted to be a part of. I was just scared once we had this amazing friendship that I'd ruin it if you didn't feel the same way. I could never leave you alone, Becca; you're my ending, no one else. I need you more than you will ever need me."

The Broken Girl

    I want to pull away because my heart can't take anymore now that it's torn in three. The love I have for my Keegan, Jake, and the new Keegan that has crept up on me. Jake just looks at me, waiting for an answer, I can't give him one I don't know myself. "Becca, I know you love him, but you love me too. Right now isn't our time, but it will be soon. Keegan will either remember or he won't, but he will still need his friends. He's going home today and he's going to need all the help he can get." I was feeling warm and fuzzy until that moment. Something in me snapped and I couldn't hold back my anger.

    "Ugh! Why does everyone keep saying that? It's not his home, it's a new place that he is all alone in when he should have been with my brother… or better yet, he shouldn't have even met me. I never should have come to Lakehead." I immediately regretted lashing out at Jake but I couldn't help it. I look back to Jake and I see he's struggling to hold back tears. "Jake, I'm sorry. I shouldn't have yelled at you." He shakes his head and I look away from this raw emotion I'm seeing from him.

    "Becca, it's not because you got upset. I understand your anger. Just… never say that again. Don't ever say you shouldn't have come here because that's what hurts. Thinking that I won't have you in my life. That's a life I'm not interested in being a part of. I will always choose you, Becca."

The emotions that I feel from his words cause my heart to go into a frenzy. I can barely catch my breath and I feel like I'm being suffocated. It's too much, too fast. I barely feel like me anymore and to hear him say all this just makes that more apparent. "Jacob, I love you, but my life is just so thoroughly screwed up right now. I just… I need some air. I will be back in a few hours, okay? I promise. I'm not trying to run out on you, so don't feel that way… I need to go and draw or something. Reconnect-to-Becca kind of deal."

He nods his head and I know he understands this more than anyone. Sometimes I just need to be alone and work through it on my own. Jake has always understood that. I gather my things and head for the door. "Where are you going though, Becca? Remember it might not be safe out there for you." I take a deep breath and try to remember that there is still this new threat that someone was after me.

"I'll be careful. I promise. Jacob…"

"Yeah, Becca?" Jake responds.

"I could never regret meeting you." I feel like I've just said more than what I

The Broken Girl

actually should have and I hope that he understands that's all I have right now.

"Me either, baby. Where are you going?"

"Solitude." I knew as soon as I said it that Jake would assume this was about Keegan. That place had become my place to go think and draw. I look to Jake and the hurt in his eyes is crippling. He must be thinking that because this was a place Keegan and I shared, that I'm going to think about Keegan. Which is true, but I'm going there because of Jake too. The longer my heart takes with all this, the more people are going to get hurt. The biggest question is: who do I love? The answer is the problem.

I love them both.

Chapter Eleven

Leaving Jake like that was not just difficult, it was unbearable. But I couldn't deal. Old Becca came out and I ran. I'm trying not to do that, but it's a habit I'm fighting everyday not to keep. Sitting here in my solitude brings me into a peaceful place in the utter chaos that has become my life. When shit gets hard, Becca flakes and it's fight or flight. Let's just say I rarely pick a fight. Being here around nature makes my life melt away. I can breathe and actually form thoughts. Jake is awake and doing well, so he will be getting released soon. Keegan, well, he doesn't remember but I will always remember for the both of us. Maybe it's a blessing for him. He doesn't have to remember all the horrible sides of our relationship. He can move on and be happy. *What about you, Becca?* Well, I honestly don't know. I love Jake, but I still love Keegan. I feel like I'm abandoning him. My brother as much as told me this and he is right. No matter the cost to my heart and

The Broken Girl

pride, I will still be his friend if that's what Keegan needs.

It's starting to get late now. It's been dark for hours, but leaving this place is like going out into a world I don't know anymore and makes me want to just stay put. Jake will be worrying though and Alec, well, he doesn't know of the threat. I am freezing so I decide to rush off to the dorm and shower. When I'm heading back to my dorm, I see the door is slightly open. My heart drops and I look around frantically then scold myself. I probably just left it open. I peek in and no one is there. I walk to my dresser and pick out a pair of jeans, grabbing my Lakehead sweater. I go to grab my phone that is charging by my bed and I stop. I look at the pillow, afraid to touch it. In front of me, just resting on my pillow, is a single black rose. Attached to it is a card and my fingers graze it.

"Soon."

I can't hold the emotions in and they come bursting out of me. I drag myself away from the bed and find the corner of the room. I had grabbed my phone on the way to the corner and already was dialing. "Hello." His voice comes to me, and then I realize I've made a mistake. "Bec, Are you there?" I have stopped correcting him because it doesn't matter anymore. I want to hang up but that would be childish.

"Sorry, Keegan, I shouldn't have called. I will call Alec." I can't hold the sobbing back and he must hear it.

"Bec, where are you? What happened?"

I am hyperventilating from the panic of hearing Keegan and the item on my pillow. I try to pull in my emotions and steady my voice. "I'm not your problem anymore. I shouldn't have called you." With that, I hang up the phone, shutting Keegan out. Or so I thought.

I'm still in the corner crying not long after when someone busts through my door. I scream, throwing my hands over my mouth. I cower, not even looking at my intruder. I feel arms around me and I shriek while trying to get myself free.

"Bec, open your eyes! It's just me!" Hearing his voice, my eyes pop open and my screams become silent. I'm trembling and the sobs coming from me are panicked. I can't catch my breath. I'm happy on one hand that he's here. Keegan came, but now he will know my secret.

"How did you find me?" My words shake out from me through my sobs.

"I was at the school when you called. I knew you lived in the dorms because your brother had told me. I started in this

The Broken Girl

direction as soon as your name displayed on my phone. I asked where your room was and someone told me the rest of the way. I don't know how I knew, but I knew you were in trouble. How can I remember that and the way your voice changes? How can I feel your panic before you even called me, but not remember you?" He brushes my hair off my face and looks so unlike the Keegan I have known.

"Bec, why did you hang up? I thought we were... I thought you came to me when things scared you or you needed someone?" I just stay still and silent for as long as possible. This isn't the Keegan I knew; this is someone new. "Bec, look at me please." I hesitate, knowing once I look into those eyes it will be over, and I will answer whatever he asks. He puts his hands under my chin and brings my eyes right to his.

"Keegan, I'm not your problem anymore." I see hurt in his eyes but I know if he remembered me I'd be staring at devastation.

"Things may be screwed up and I may not remember you here." He points to his head. "But that doesn't mean I don't care because as much as I don't understand it, I remember you here." His hand falls just over his heart. "Bec, I will always come when you call. I'm not going anywhere. You promised no matter what, you'd hold me to being friends."

I don't know what to say to Keegan. He has never been like this before so I just nod. "Now tell me, Bec, what has you in knots and shaking?" I peek over to my pillow and he follows my gaze. He gets up and walks to my bed, picking up the black rose with the attached card. "Soon? Bec, what the fuck is this? Is this left over from Dillon?" I shake my head than tell him everything.

"No, one, because it's not dead just painted black. Two, it wasn't here when I went to the shower and when I came back my door wasn't closed properly. Three, well, this isn't the first message I've gotten since Dillon died. Since he's not around, I think I have another problem."

I finally look at him and he doesn't look at all pleased by my sarcasm. "Don't be a smartass. Who knows about all this? "I shake my head because, until recently, no one knew until Jake saw the note. "Fine. What other messages?" I pull myself together before trying to speak.

"He may not have finished the job but I will." His eyes turn from rage to fear. He goes to put his arms out for me, but lets them fall back to his side. "I found the note in my dorm while you were all in the

The Broken Girl

hospital. I thought someone was just screwing with me but now I'm not so sure."

"Bec, you can't stay here tonight. Come back to my place." A part of me wants to jump to that offer but I shake my head.

"That's not a good idea, Keegan, and you know it." He looks worried but then smirks. "Either go to your brother's or you are coming home with me, good idea or not." Keegan has always been sexy, but this attitude is something he never showed me. He treated me like a fragile doll and I guess with good reason but he's got me so worked up. He's just looking at me now. I stir at the way he's looking at me, trying to think of anything else but his hands on me.

"I'm going to call Drake and Charlotte to come get me. Drake isn't too happy with you so it's probably a good idea if you leave first." He nods and I make the call. They tell me they will be here in 10 minutes. I tell them nothing about this.

"Keegan, don't tell anyone. I don't want anyone to freak out. I will tell them if it happens again." A lie. I know if I don't have to tell anyone, I won't. It's time I handle things on my own.

"I won't keep this secret forever, Bec. If I think they need to know, I will tell them and you can be pissed at me all you want."

I thank him and wait for him to leave. He walks over to the door but stops at my dresser. There is a picture of him and I just before Christmas. We look so happy as if we don't have a care in the world. Things had just started to get good for us then. "We look happy."

I walk up and take the picture from him. "We were, Keegan. Remember we were friends too. That's not going to change."

I look at him to see he is staring at my necklace. "I must have loved you to give you this. It's my grandmother's."

This is news to me. I go to take it off but he stops me. "No, I want you to have it. I gave it to you for a reason obviously." I shake my head and try to get it off again. "Things have changed and this should be with you for someone you spend your life with."

"We don't know that this isn't still going to happen for us, Bec. So please keep it." He goes to the door and opens it slightly before stopping. I see him struggling with his emotions but when he speaks, I am stunned.

"All the shrinks say it's my brains way of dealing with it all. I may not remember you in every aspect. But I remember your smell, the way my body reacts when it touches you. I know it wants you; a part of

The Broken Girl

me does too. This is just so fucked up. God, they said it wouldn't be damn easy, but damn it, they never told me it feels like I was having my heart ripped out every time I have to walk away from you." With that, he pulls the door the rest of the way open and leaves me sitting here thinking.

Who the hell is that? How do I love him already? My new Keegan, all screwed up, not knowing which way to go.

Chapter Twelve

"Becca, are you alright?" I look at Drake, who came up to get me while Charlotte waits in the car.

"I just need to get back to the hospital. Jake's probably wondering where I am?" By the look on Drake's face he's probably called Drake a number of times already. "I went for a walk and I just lost track of time." He nods at me and grabs me for a hug. I feel him tense and I realize the rose is still on my bed. I pull back and he's staring at it. I pull back and follow his line of sight to the rose. "I have an admirer." I was trying to play it off as a joke, but I can tell he's not buying it. Drake doesn't want to call me out on it right now. However, I know he will be keeping a closer eye on me from now on. To be honest, that's probably a good thing. Someone is definitely after me or, at the very least, trying to scare me into leaving. They might just win and get what they want. I might just leave Lakehead.

The Broken Girl

"Drake, have you ever regretted something that you could still change?" He looks taken aback by what I've said but I wait for his answer.

"Becca, I regret how I treated you and how I went out of my way to make your life a living hell." I just nod because I know he means this. I say what I've been thinking since I was in the Netherlands.

"I regret coming to Lakehead." I hear him gasp and I look away from him.

"So what are you going to do?"

I take a deep breath and try to keep my voice as calm as possible. "I'm going to finish this year, but next year I will start applying to art schools in Europe." I feel Drake's hand on my shoulder and I know he's trying to comfort me. "Don't tell anyone please, Drake. I only told my parents I'd do my two years here so then I could go to art school. This is what I planned to do before any of this."

When we get back to the hospital, I give both Drake and Charlotte hugs, but tell them to go off and enjoy the night. I make my way to Jake's room and I find Alec in there. "Jake, man, I don't know what's going to happen with Becca. You and Keegan are my friends but she's my sister. I won't make the

~ 94 ~

same mistake again. I will protect her above all. So remember that."

I make a loud noise as I open the door they both look at me and I just smile. "Hey, Alec, what are you still doing here?" It's late and he's usually gone by this time.

"I was waiting for you, Becca. Where did you go?" I walk up and give him a hug, squeezing him tightly.

"Went for a run." I started running again after the accident to clear my head so he's not going to question me. "Well, I will let you two hang out. I'll see you in the morning."

As soon as Alec is out the door Jake is moving over so I can climb in with him. "They told me I could leave tomorrow morning."

I look to Jake and give him the biggest smile I can. "Jake, that's great! I can't wait to get back to the dorms." He looks saddened by my excitement.

"I'm not going back to the dorms, not yet anyway. I will stay with Alec for a bit. Easier to have everything I need like an adjoining bathroom and my own shower." I didn't expect to have to go back to my brother's yet. Charlotte is staying in my room, not that I wouldn't just room with Jake. "I will still see you all the time." Just like that, my heart drops and my whole body

The Broken Girl

goes tense. I look to him for clarification, anything to tell me he's not saying what I think he is.

He doesn't say anything else, he just looks at me. I give him a hug and kiss his cheek, holding in every tear that wants to erupt from my body. "I'll see you later Jake." I go to walk away and he tries to grab for me. "I better get home, it's getting late. I have classes in the morning. When you get out, let me know if you need any help." I turn my back to Jake and the tears begin to fall.

"Becca, please just stay, just for tonight." Those words break me. He's ending this. I don't know what changed between our last talk and now but he's made up his mind.

"No, Jacob, I need to go home. One more night won't change this. It won't make this feel any less than it does now. Right now, it's killing me. So thanks but no thanks. Goodbye." With that, I'm out of the door and running down the halls, trying to get as far away from this place as possible.

I get outside and call a cab. While I wait, I replay things over and over, trying to figure out if I was misunderstanding Jake. *He doesn't want you to stay with him, Becca.* The cab pulls up and I hop in without worrying about it. I am trying to keep it together the entire way home to my dorm, alone. As soon as we pull up, I toss some money on the seat and take off to my room. I rush past Jake's door and slam mine, causing the wall to shake. I peel off all my clothing, trying to get the smell of Jake off of me. I pull my PJs on and don't bother locking my door. I wish whomever it was that wants to hurt me would just do it already. I'm not playing this game anymore. I climb into my bed and fall into a sleep I hope I never wake from.

Trees, dirt, and the smell of burnt rubber begin to fill my head. My eyes blink open and I see my surroundings. I'm on the road where I was just a few short weeks ago. I see the car mangled and the air is filled with silence. "Becky." I turn to see both Dillon and Michael standing there staring at me. Dillon looks like he did before we started dating. He appears normal.

"What's happening?" I look to Michael, who is now walking towards me.

"Bec, this is what you do." I'm confused and I'm sure he can tell by my face. "You cause damage where ever you go."

I begin to sob at his hateful words and I can't even speak. I just keep shaking my head no. "I died because of you. Because you were selfish, and then you drove Dillon insane. Then you did the worst thing possible."

The Broken Girl

"NO!" I scream at them.

"Where are Jake and Keegan? They couldn't be safe around you either, could they, Becca?"

I'm trembling when I get my next words out. "Where are Keegan and Jake? What did you do to them? Don't hurt them!"

Dillon looks at me with sadness. "Becky, we wouldn't hurt them. They left on their own, remember?"

Flashes of my conversation with Jake and the heartbreak of it come crashing down. Keegan not having his memories of the last year and a half. I look to Dillon and I see sadness.

"Keegan doesn't want to remember you and Jake can't be around you, Becca. They are gone and you're alone. Why would they want to be around someone who's only going to get them killed?"

"I would never hurt them! I love them. I wouldn't let them get hurt!" I'm screaming and I feel like I'm being shaken. "You're a killer, Becca. You may not have done it yourself with me, but you did kill Dillon and you will get them killed."

I scream and feel like I'm being pulled away from all this.

"Becca, wake up!"

I feel the pull getting stronger and before I know it.

"BECCA!!!" My eyes spring open and I see Drake looking at me. "Did you take anything?"

I shake my head and the sobs begin to burst out of me. "Drake." He grabs me and gives me a hug.

"Jake called me, Becca. You should have called Charlotte or I would have stayed with you." I pull away, shaking my head. "No, Drake, no more of this. I'm not going to be this broken girl anymore. I need to start to put back together the pieces of my life and I need to be able to do it alone. It's time for me to handle my own shit and fight my own demons."

The Broken Girl

Chapter Thirteen

    Keep busy. That's my thoughts these days. Waking up to Drake trying to take care of me gave me this kick in the ass I so desperately needed. I have slept soundly by myself for five days. Well, soundly might not be the right term. I've been taking my medication for sleeping. So I don't wake anyone screaming, but it doesn't stop the nightmares. Jake has been home at Alec's place for all of those nights. I haven't been there and I'm not returning anyone's calls except Charlotte. Alec is of course panicking that I'm going to take off. Charlotte told him I'm not leaving and she's right. I'm not leaving… yet. I grab my bag from my desk and head out into the world I've been trying to evade.
    Walking to my class, I wish I could say it was getting easier to be here. The truth is that each day I walk around here, it is killing me. I've begun to hate it here. I don't talk to anyone. I stay away from the group. To be honest, I haven't spoken to anyone. Jake

hasn't tried to come see me either. I was hoping he would come around, but he seems to enjoy the distance. Making my way to the library, it has become my safe zone.

"Bec…" I still at Keegan's voice and turn around. He's alone at least, which means this will be less awkward.

"Hello, Keegan, how are you?" He looks at me questioningly.

"I'm good," he responds.

"That's good. I better get going. I have to study." I turn away and start to my getaway.

"Really, Bec, that's all I get?" I don't turn around, and I don't stop either. *Keep walking, Becca.* "Rebecca!"

I stop in my tracks and turn slowly, looking at Keegan. "What do you want from me, Keegan?" I say to him, with tears pooling in my eyes. Keegan looks back and forth down the halls before he approaches me. He grabs me by the arm and starts pulling me out of the school and along the path to our solitude. I haven't been back here since the night I left Jake at the hospital.

Keegan still hasn't let go of me. I try to pull and struggle against him. "Bec, if you don't cut that shit out right now…" I break free of his grasp and go to take off again. Thinking I'm actually getting away from Keegan was my first mistake. "Have it your

The Broken Girl

way, Becca." He scoops me up throwing me over his shoulder.

"Keegan, put me down!" I scream.

"Fuck that shit. You aren't getting out of this we have some serious shit to talk about." With Keegan's response, I give up the fight. I know I won't be able to get away from him. Keegan continues to carry me up the path until we have reached our spot. He sets me down on the rock formation and I don't bother trying to get away this time.

"Okay, you have me where you want me, so how about you tell me what the hell you want from me?

Keegan puts his hands up in the air with frustration. "Cut the shit, Bec, it's not cute."

"Being cute? Why, it got me into this fricking mess? I just want to walk around, go to my classes, finish the semester, and leave!" The words are out of my mouth before I can stop them; I look to the ground hoping it will open up and swallow me whole.

Keegan stomps right up to me and brings his hands to my face. "Leave? What the hell does that mean?"

"Keegan, I have to, I need too. I'm going to finish what I said I would. I'm going to be done with my first year soon. Charlotte wants to take me away for the summer and then I'm coming back for my final year here. I will be transferring to an art school after that. I promised my dad I'd do two years and then I would go to art school. I'm going to try talking him into it at the end of the semester again. Maybe he will let me start this September instead of doing another year. If not, I will do what I promised; you will all be graduating that year anyway. But at some point I have to do what's right for me." Keegan looks overloaded with the information I've giving him.

"No, Becca, you can't leave at the end of this year. You have to stay. Alec needs you and so does Jake." He still hasn't let go of my face.

"They will be fine, Jake and I aren't even talking. It will be better this way for them and for me." With that, Keegan lets go of my face and spins around, taking a few steps away from me.

"What about me, Becca?" I see that his shoulders are tense.

"You will be fine too. I'm a phone call away. Besides, it might be better for you too."

"Screw that, you're running away. If that's what you want I guess I can't stop you."

The Broken Girl

Keegan's words feel like ice. "Keegan please, just let me go."

He turns to me with his eyes full of sadness. "I need you, Becca, I won't be fine. I won't be better off without you here."

"Keegan..." At this moment, I'm barely keeping it together.

"I wish I could give you what you want, because this is killing me. Becca, please stay. Fine, go away with Charlotte if that's what you want, but don't stay away. Come back give me that time. Help me remember. We all need you Becca. There is a party tonight at one of the teammate's houses. Come out. I know I'd love to see you having fun and I know Alec would too." The old Keegan never would have been this open and raw with me. It's refreshing and scaring my heart at the same time.

Keegan walks over to me. "Let me walk you back, Becca. You have a party to get ready for."

***

Standing in front of my mirror, I'm not sure how I feel about the outfit. Charlotte came over to help me get ready. I was thankful until I saw what she brought me to wear. Looking down, I see the silver miniskirt, which is barely covering anything. My legs look longer than they actually are and the pink sparkling six inch heels help with that. She gave me a matching pink sparkling halter-top to wear with it. It has no back to it and dips in the front, only being held together with a small silver pin at my breasts. My hair is pinned back and cascading in loose curls all the way down my back.

"Becca, you look amazing. Stop being self-conscious and get your purse. It's time to party." Charlotte is all decked out in a green dress that is as short as my skirt. It isn't as low cut as my top but still revealing. Her hair is straight and she's wearing a pair of shiny black heels. She looks like she just walked off a runway and has no problem showing her confidence. " Let's go then." I exhale and walk out the door, following Charlotte.

Drake is downstairs waiting for us, and his mouth drops open when he sees us coming. "Well, aren't I just a lucky son of a bitch." He wears a smirk on his face. "Charlotte, you are beautiful." All I see is that he is completely into my cousin. He adores her and her face says it's a mutual thing. "Thank you, Drake. You're looking very sexy tonight." This conversation is making me want to look away, but I can't say she's wrong. Drake's hair has some gel

The Broken Girl

in it; he's wearing a black button-up shirt with a pair of dark slim jeans. "Becca... I don't even know what to say, you just look amazing. Jake and Keegan might not know what's what, but every other guy at this party is going to want you on their arm." He winks at me and I smile softy.

When we pull up, all the confidence that I have been telling myself I had vanishes. There are people everywhere. The house has a wraparound porch and there's a keg sitting right out in the open. This party is in full swing. I see Sarah first. She was talking to a group of girls and she stopped as soon as she sees me. Drake puts his other arm around me. He starts walking with me to the porch. When we go to pass Sarah, she comes out in front of me. "Look what that cat dragged in. So Jake and Keegan released the nothing-but-a-little-attention-seeker. "Poor Becca" isn't working anymore so you've moved on to Drake." Sarah looks to Charlotte, and I can see her clenching her fist. "Better watch out that this little skank doesn't steal your man."

Charlotte lunges, but I grab her. Drake is still holding on to me protectively. "She's not worth it, Charlotte." I try to get through to her.

"You are right, Becca, she isn't." She turns to Sarah, looking her right in the eye. "Besides, I have the joy of knowing my cousin Becca threw your dumbass out of the apartment... In your undies, no less. That's all I need. I bet you looked like the attention seeking whore you are." With that, Charlotte turns and grabs me as we walk around a stunned Sarah. "Next time I'm punching her in the face, Becca." I laugh because I'm not sure what else to do. I know Charlotte would do it and the best part of it is that I'd love to see it.

Drake takes us around back and sets us up on some loungers. He goes to get us some drinks and tell my brother we are here. I look around and I spot Jake with Kristy, laughing. He turns, but I look away before he can see me watching him. Seeing him with her brought it all back. I know he's not doing it to hurt me but the sight of it has re-broken my broken heart. Drake looks at me, having seen the hurt in my face. He comes and sits next to me and puts himself in front of something. I look around him and see Keegan with Sarah now. "Becca, I promise they are idiots."

"No, I am the idiot. I lost the two people I loved because I couldn't choose." I got up and began to walk away. They got up to follow but I just shake my head and they

The Broken Girl

realize I just need to be alone. I walk off to the other side of the backyard, by the fire. I just look into the fire wishing it had the answers. If only I hadn't fallen in love with both of them. If I could have just chose one. They say that if you fall in love with someone else, then you let the first one go. You didn't love them as much as you thought or you wouldn't have fallen in love with the second person… My problem is this, which person did I love first? That's the question.

"Your friend thought you could use a drink." I look up and see a guy I've seen around the team before, but I don't know him. I look to where he's pointing and I see my brother with Keegan, Charlotte, and Drake. Sarah is also there with her hands around Keegan. The sight makes me thankful there is a drink being handed to me. I grab it from him, thanking him and send cheers to my group of friends who are also doing the same. I down the drink in seconds. Glancing over, I see Keegan, Drake, and my brother staring at me like I've grown a second head. "That was much needed, thank you." I get up and walk away. The last thing I need is another guy in my life.

Well, trying to get out of the watchful eyes of my friends, I bump right into someone. "Becca." I don't have to look to know who it is.

"Sorry, Jake, I wasn't watching where I was going." I go to move around him, I can't do this right now.

"Becca, no, wait."

Without thinking, I turn to him. My filter I had been working so hard to keep has vanished. "Why? So you can tell me to give you space. I got that message loud and clear when you moved out of the dorms. When you left me broken. You broke me, Jake." Spinning around, I try to leave since I'm starting to feel that drink I downed. I feel his arms on me and I feel heat at the contact. God, I've missed him touching me.

"Becca, it is because you were with Keegan."

Wait?

What?

"I wasn't with him, I ended it. If you decided to walk away, know it's because of you. I know what I want, Jake." Jake looks at me and I know whatever he's about to say isn't going to help matters.

"Because he couldn't remember you. You fought so hard to stay with him and keep things with you two." I'm stunned. Did he hear nothing I said to him in the hospital? I'm too mad to hold anything back.

"You can't blame me for staying. I ran

The Broken Girl

to you with everything and you always said the right things to send me back! You told me you didn't love me like that. YOU DID IT TO ME. It broke my heart every goddamn time. I didn't know it then. I didn't know that you had stolen my heart but every time you did the "I'm not in love with you," I felt it. You broke me, Jacob Kelso. You pushed me towards him. You smiled when he did sweet things; you encouraged me to give him another chance! Now you saying you blame me and pushed me away now because of that. Don't you get it? Jake… I loved you. Always you. Maybe you just didn't love me like you think. Now you're blaming me for not sharing my feelings! When you couldn't tell me either like that's fair. Well, that's bullshit, Jake." I turn and begin to walk away.

"Becca, wait! Please." The change in his voice makes me still instantly but I don't turn around. "Becca, you think any of that was easy for me. I was doing it because I thought he made you happy. I would do anything to make you happy. I'd even hide my own love for you. Every time I told you I wasn't in love with you, it was like my heart was being crushed against my chest. Saying those words was the second hardest thing I ever did. Every time I said I love you,

I meant it. I love you more than anything. In my head, when I'd say I love you, all the things I love about you would follow it. All I thought about was this sad girl I found in the front of the school. I loved you the moment you gave me that shy awkward wave in the café the day we met. This unbelievable shy, beautiful girl had so much to offer the world, but wouldn't open up. I wanted to be that person. It was just that you didn't just need me. I wasn't enough. Keegan wasn't enough either. That girl will have everything she ever needs. She just can't see it right now. She loved so openly, but never let those love her back. I'm not going to be enough for you now. That's why…"

    I interrupt him before he can finish. I know what's coming, but I love him. Why is he doing this to me? "Jake, please, I'm begging you, don't do this." I feel his hand touch the back of my hair and I still won't turn to him. I can't. "Want to know the hardest thing I ever had to do? The one thing that surpasses telling you I wasn't in love with you… it was telling you to stay in the dorms and not come home with me. But it was the right thing to do." I can't stand this anymore. My heart is crashing against the walls of my chest; I do what 'Becca' always does. Which means I run. Going right into the house, away from Jake and everyone I

The Broken Girl

care about. Not stopping until I'm upstairs and find myself locked in the bathroom. I lock the door and sink to the ground.

Why can't he just see that I love him? Why does he have to not see that I run to him because of that? He was always enough for me. I just didn't think he wanted me. Tears that were pooling in my eyes have now found their way down my cheeks, falling to the floor under me. I feel this fog come over me. "What was that drink?" My words are slow. Something isn't right. Grabbing the door handle, I try to get up but my body is slow to reply. The bathroom is spinning. Something is happening to me. Finally, I make it up and get out the door. People are coming up the stairs. I know I should ask for help but I don't know what's happening. My only thought is to find Jake. I feel like I'm dying. I can't let that be the last thing I've said to him. Making my way to the bottom of the stairs, I see Jake. "Jake." My eyes are barely staying open. He turns and sees me but just turns again and walks right out the front door. My heart sinks. If I could actually fathom what just happened, my world may have actually stopped.

Using the wall to guide me, I try to find someone who I trust before I finally collapse. I see a room that looks like and office.

There's someone in there and even from behind, I know who it is. He's looking at something on the wall. I get in the door and almost make it to him. I feel the room spinning out of control. I can't take another step. Just as I feel my body shutting down, I call out to the one person I trust as much as Jake, "Keegan."

Chapter Fourteen

Keegan

Standing in the hall, I see Jake and Becca talking. I know I shouldn't be listening to this because, man, it's fucking with my heart right now. "The one thing that surpasses telling you I wasn't in love with you… it was telling you to stay in the dorms and not come home with me. But it was the right thing to do." I can't believe that dumbass just said that to Bec. Watching her reaction, she takes off, not letting him do any more damage to her. Once she's gone, I want to go after her, but I just stand there. Jake turns and sees me. "What, Key? Got something to say?"

I move up to him and get right into his face. "Yeah, I do, man. I don't know who you fucking are right now. You never would talk to a girl like that before. That was overly harsh and you know it." He takes a step back from me. "You don't know what the hell you're talking about, Key, so go find a lock to pick at and leave me the hell alone. Don't you think you've done enough?" I feel bad because I don't remember all what I've done, but I know I'm to blame for some of this too.

"Shit, Jake, from what I'm told it is my job to be the fuck up. Let's not try to put me out of a job, would you?" With that, I turn and go in search of Becca. I don't know how I know this but she needs me right now.

I search all over the house for her but I can't seem to find her. Maybe she left. Well, walking back to get a drink, I saw this painting in the office. It looks so much like this spot I found when I first came here. I just stare at it. I duck in so I don't have to go back to Sarah and I just wanted to get away from her. Man, she just had to keep her hands on me. It just didn't feel the way it used to. I find myself wondering that more and more. A few nights ago, we had actually had done some heavy fooling around for the first time since my accident. I'd had a bunch to drink with the team, and ran into her on my way home. I don't remember much, but it didn't feel right. There's a noise behind me, but I don't turn since it's probably Sarah. Maybe if I ignore her she will just keep going and not bother me.

The Broken Girl

"Keegan." The hairs on the back of my neck stand up. Turning around, I already know something is wrong.

"Bec!" Before I can make it to her, she collapsed on the floor. "Bec, wake up." I'm grabbing her cheeks, trying to get her to look at me. I pick her up and bring her to the couch in the office. She slacks in my arms. Looking around frantically, I don't know what to do. Should I call 911? I check her pulse. She appears to have fainted but that doesn't make sense. Maybe she had too much to drink?

Grabbing my cell, I pull out my phone and call Jake. I don't want to call 911 if she's just drunk and get her into trouble. I will take care of her if that's all this is. "Jake, it's Becca." He is silent for a minute. It feels like forever.

"I told you, Key, I'm not talking about it. Bye."

"Wait." I yell into the phone.

"What the hell, Key?" he yells back at me.

"Do you know how much she had to drink? I think she's wasted." I ask quietly.

"She didn't have anything when she was around me or when I saw her. She usually only has one or two. Nice try, Key,

Gracie Wilson

I'm not falling for it, bye." He hung up on me. That fucking jackass!

I quickly dial him back. "WHAT!" He roars into the phone. "Get your head out of your ass and come to the office in the back of the house and come alone. Something's wrong with Becca. She passed out." I hang up on him, serves him right, he can panic now. Looking down at her, she just appears to be sleeping. "No, it can't be?" I say to myself. There's no way, it can't be. I hear the door bust open and I turn around to see Jake standing in the doorway.

"Close the door." He does as I ask and then runs over to Becca but I stand in his path. "So now you care about her. Now that she is in actual trouble. No, maybe you should just go. She doesn't need you; I'll take care of her. Remember, you are walking away. So just do it." I knew I had gone too far, but I never expected Jake to punch me.

"We don't have time for this, Key. Call 911."

I get up to see him checking her. "She's going to be fine."

He gets up and pushes me out of the way and goes to grab his phone that has fallen on the floor. I panic because I know if she ends up in the hospital and her parents find out, then that's it for Bec being here.

The Broken Girl

"No, stop. Don't call. She's fine. She got some of the party favours in her drink." I'm hoping by saying it this way that he won't kill me when he finds out I knew that this was going on at the party.

"You're telling me you know she's been drugged, but haven't called 911. Are you that fucking thick headed or are you just trying to save your own ass from the cops?" Something in me snaps and I knock him right in the jaw.

"No, I'm saying if we take her in they will just keep her for observation and her brother or her parents find out they will take her back home. You know how much she doesn't want that, I'm sure. Not to mention that the giant screw up that you have become won't get a chance to wake the fuck up and realize he's being a shithead."

"You knew about the drugs and didn't say anything. What the hell is wrong with you? Who the hell are you, Key?" The way Jake is looking at me right now is full of disapproval. Unfortunately, he's right. Who am I? Looking over, I see this girl I can't quite remember, but my heart seems to cling to.

"Who had the drugs, Key?" I can't seem to look away from her; I just want to hold her. "Key!"

~ 118 ~

"Sarah and some of the guys from school." Fuck! My heart is pounding in my chest.

Just then, Charlotte walks through the door. "Guys, have you seen Becca?" As soon as Charlotte sees her, I know what's coming. "What is wrong with her. Did she drink too much?" I can't look at her, so I don't. "Key, are you going to tell her or are you going to make me do it?"

I haven't moved or said a word. My eyes can't seem to move from Bec. "Fine, someone brought drugs to the party and Becca had some. Guess she's branching out."

"What did you just say, Jake?" I have to be imagining that he would think this. "You think she took them?"

Jake turns and looks at me, causing him to maybe get an idea of what I'm trying to say. I stand up and walk away from Bec and get close to him. "You think that's who she is? I can't remember her and I'm not even that fucking stupid enough to think that. Someone had put it in her drink. I only saw her with one drink and she downed it." Jake becomes pale and backs away from me.

"Jake, you think she would take drugs willingly? Aren't you supposed to be Becca's best friend?" Charlotte is looking at Jake like he's a dog who just shit on her carpet.

The Broken Girl

"So Charlotte doesn't know what an ass you've been to her or how you told her you were done with her." Charlotte looks horrified. I know this isn't the time, but I can't stop my anger since he doesn't seem to know her at all. I would give anything to remember every detail about her and he just gave up on her. If she is who I believe she is, I wouldn't give a damn who was in my way. "It wasn't enough for Jacob to move out and stop being the person she runs to. Then tonight, after we all begged her to come, you do that to her. What is wrong with you?"

"Keegan, is she going to be okay?" Charlotte is watching me. I walk over to Bec and move a few strands of her long hair out of her face. "Get Sarah. We need to know what was in that drink." Charlotte goes to leave, but I stop her.

"No, she won't come with you, Charlotte. Jake, you go get her." Jake doesn't move. "I don't think that's a good idea."

"I wasn't asking, Jake." He reluctantly leaves in search of Sarah. "Keegan, tell me she's going to be okay." I look to her and give her the only answer I can, the only one I can believe. "Yes, Charlotte, she's going to be fine." I hope.

Jake is bringing Sarah in and, as soon as she sees Bec, she tries to turn around and leave. "No, you don't bitch. What the hell did my cousin get?" Charlotte is pissed I can't blame her. I want to yell at her too. For some reason, I don't think this was just a mistake.

"Key, there you are. Come on baby, let's go." Sarah looks to me, hoping I will save her, but that's not going to fucking happen.

"Sarah, don't be cute. What the hell was in the party favours tonight?" She just looks at me pouting. "Sarah!"

"Fine, okay, calm down. It's not my fault she took some." Sarah just stands there as if she actually believes it. "What was it tonight, Sarah?" I ask her, trying to sound sweet and unaffected.

"God, fine, it was GHB." I want to scream at her, scare the living shit out of her, but I have to remain calm if I want to get all I can out of her.

"Sarah, I get it. You just wanted her to have a right time, babe. She's been down and you wanted her to have fun at the party." I'm asking her something I already suspect. Jake and Charlotte are looking at me like I've lost my mind.

"Babe, you know me. I just wanted her to loosen up. She needed to have a little fun."

The Broken Girl

I don't get the chance to do or say anything before I see Charlotte's fist connect to Sarah's face.

"You stupid bitch." Sarah has a bloody lip and is walking towards Charlotte with a look that says this isn't the end. "Sarah, enough."

"Key, baby, she hit me."

I am seething now. "Why, Sarah? Just tell me why you put it in her drink." She takes a step back from Charlotte; I almost want her to go for Charlotte because I bet she would lay her ass out right here in this office.

"Why? Because she's sniffing around what's mine. I just wanted her to be out of the way for tonight so we could be together. You're always looking at her and staring at her. I just wanted you to myself. She doesn't get that you are mine. She didn't get it then and she doesn't get it now."

I take a step, closing the difference between us. "So you drugged her to get her out of the way. What the fuck is wrong with you? Sarah, that's low, even for you. I can't look at you. I don't want to see you! You get out of here before I change my mind and call the police and report you. I'm done with your crazy shit."

"It's all your fault that I had to do this. If you could just stop watching her and wanting her. What is it with that bitch that makes you all run to her? If you'd just let her go, I'd never have done this. So don't be all high and mighty. She's laying there because of you." With that, Sarah storms out, leaving me with Jake and Charlotte.

"Keegan, we can't tell Alec. He will tell her parents and she won't survive being brought back home right now. I'm all she has right now and I've started some night classes." Jake and I both wince at the dig Charlotte has just given both of us. "Can you guys get along and take care of her like she has tried to do for both of you. I will go and make sure Alec and Drake do not come looking for her tonight. Text me updates on her." We both nod. It's not as if we can disagree with her. Charlotte leaves us and I don't even look at Jake. I walk up to the couch and lift her head softly and sit down, laying her head on my lap.

"This is all my fault. If I had been able to find her or stayed with her, this wouldn't have happened. What if she hadn't been able to find me?" Jake isn't saying anything to me, not that I expected an answer. "Bec, please be okay." If she isn't… I can't even think about that.

The Broken Girl

"Key, stop it. She found you at least you helped her. No matter how fucked up your head is, you didn't turn your back on her."

Something in his voice made me question what he was saying. I slip out from under her, resting her head back on the couch and come up behind Jake. "What's that supposed to mean? Jake, what aren't you saying?"

"She came down the stairs and she called out to me. I walked away."

I don't even think when he turns and looks at me.

I swing, going down with him.
My fist connects. Twice.

"Don't stop, I deserve it." I get off him.

"You're right, you do, but I figure my fists will hurt less than the guilt that you walked away when she needed you."

"God, she will never forgive me for this. I just didn't want to fight any more. It was killing me to be away from her and she just wouldn't get it. I just walked away. I didn't know she was in trouble. Fuck if I did. I'd never have walked away from her, no matter how hard it is to be close to her."

I want to hit him again, but I understand some of what he is saying.

~ 124 ~

"Jake, just go. I will take care of her. Just go, okay? I will take care of her. If you stay, I might beat the shit out of you. I won't tell Alec or anyone else, but you will have to tell Bec." Jake looks hesitant about it but he knows he doesn't have room to argue. I'm letting him off, but Alec won't. He gets up and goes to her. I want to stop him, but I just watch.

"Becca, I love you, please don't hate me tomorrow." He kisses her head and leaves without looking at me. "Call me if you need help. I'll be back tomorrow to… talk to her."

The party seems to have died down and I figure I should see if I could get her a bed upstairs somewhere. I open the door and check the hall. Going back into the office, I pick her up and carry her in my arms. To anyone she will just look asleep and tired. They will think she's drunk. But that's better than everyone thinking she's been drugged. Making our way upstairs, no one really notices anything. I'm sure they are all thinking we are together still or again. Who knows? I don't care what anyone thinks, as long as it's not negative about Bec. Opening one of the doors, I find one of the first years on the team in the room getting hot and heavy against a chair in the corner. "Out." He looks up and sees it's me. No questions, he grabs his girl and leaves. I bring her to

The Broken Girl

the bed and maneuver her in my arms so I can pull back the blankets. Putting her down, I go back and close the door locking it.

"What have I done?" I turn to see her in the bed looking so unlike the girl I've fallen in love with. Again… I think. I think I loved her before my accident. I'm sure of it and I love her now too. Looking at her like this, I can't stop myself. I pull back the blankets on the other side and climb in with her. She may kill me tomorrow. But my fear that I will never remember holding her is overwhelming and this is my only chance. As I cuddle into her, I feel her heat against me. It feels normal, but it makes my heart beat faster. I bring her head and lay it on my chest. Her hand moves and she grabs onto my shirt. My heart stops. Maybe she's waking up. I look down at her but she's still out cold.

"Bec, please forgive me. I'm so sorry." I bring my hand into her hair and she smells like home. My heart feels at home with her. The memories seem to be just within my reach but I can't seem to get them back. My heart remembers this and her, but not my brain. Lowering my head to her, I kiss the top of her head. I'm overcome with these damn emotions. I don't know what to do with them. I want to scream and yell at

Sarah. But she was right. I am drawn to Bec, and I watch her constantly. I think about her always. Wondering if she's different after the accident. Either way, I bet I would still love this girl.

"I love you, Bec. I'm so sorry this happened to you. If something had happened to you or if someone had done something to you… Fuck. I love you." Holding her tightly, I cling to the hope that she will forgive me and that I won't lose everything I am desperately craving. "I will do whatever it takes to be in your life, and I will never turn away from you. If you call or need me, I'm yours. Forever."

I give into these fucking emotions. "Why can't I remember you? Now you're never going to want me. I need you Bec." I continue thinking to myself how can God be this fucking cruel. To make me crave her, need her, but unable to remember the one thing I can't seem to live without.

"I want you to wake up so badly, but if you do, you won't let me hold you. That will fucking kill me. I already feel like I can't breathe at the damn thought of not being like this with you ever again. Just give me a chance, Bec? My mind forgot you, but my heart is dying to have you. I won't get through losing you." I can't even remember what I'd be losing, but I know it would be

The Broken Girl

the death of me. I'd give anything to have her in my life still. Even if she never lets me touch her like this, even if I never remember her again, because I'd give up everything to see her happy. Even if that means it's not with me.

The thought of her being with someone else is like a sharp knife into my heart. I want all of her. She already has all of me. I didn't know it then but when I woke up, it was still all there. The thought of the fact that I've done something that ended up harming her and the fact that I know this is going to make her cry breaks me apart. It rips my heart wide open. The pain is unbearable. It continues to beat through the pain, even though I'd give anything to have it stop so that I could never cause this girl any more hurt.

The walls I'd built up so many years ago, the ones I have been desperately trying to keep up when she walked into my life and crashed into me, slowly break. I sob while cuddling into this girl who has taken over my heart without me knowing.

"I love you." I just keep repeating it. While I let go of all the emotions I'm feeling, I try to enjoy this moment.

Because now I might lose her forever.

Chapter Fifteen

Becca

My eyes flutter open. I feel weird. My body is sluggish and stiff. My mind is frazzled and a bit foggy. Great. To deal with my feelings, I got hammered. Good Job, Becca. I begin to take in my surroundings while never moving.

Oh! Someone is in the bed with me. I'm lying on their chest. What did I do? What happened last night? Going to bed with someone else, Becca? How pathetic can it get?

When my brain finally wakes up, I know the smell. My heart stops the racing it began as soon as I felt I wasn't alone in the bed. Did we? I feel tears come to my eyes. Not again! Why can't we have something beautiful that isn't tainted. I move slightly and he stirs. Closing my eyes tightly, I pray, hoping he will think I'm still asleep and leave. Let me do this walk of shame without having to talk to him.

The Broken Girl

"Bec? Are you awake?"

I still at the sound of his voice. Something is wrong with his tone, and it tells me this is about to get a lot worse.

"Keegan." I go to pull away, to look at him, but he holds me still. "Just stay like this for a few minutes. Please just don't leave. Just stay with me like this for a little bit longer. I'm not ready for everything to change yet." Oh, Keegan. He brings his face down to me and brings his face into my hair, cradling me in his arms. He's acting like I'm going to crash and break down. I begin to think he's protecting me when I feel the wetness that just landed on my check. Keegan is crying. I want to pull away and beg him to talk to me but I know he needs this.

"Keegan, we will get through this. Whatever this is. I promise you."

He squeezes me tightly and I feel him smelling my hair. Just as quickly as the peace has come over my heart with his closeness, he slips out from under me and is pacing in the room. "Keegan, I'm sorry. I must have had too much to drink. I'm sorry you had to take care of me. Forgive me for my drunken stupor." I'm hoping he will lose some of the tension I see in him but this only makes him stiffen.

~ 130 ~

Gracie Wilson

"Bec, don't. Please don't ask me to forgive you. Don't say you're sorry. I did this. This is entirely my fault. I want you to forgive me, but I don't deserve it." Confirmation no longer needed. We had sex and now he knows I don't remember. Why is our life so tragic that nothing can go right for us?

"Keegan. Please come here." The desperation in my words is so apparent that he gives in without me having to beg him further. He comes back to the bed and sits beside me. He looks so crushed and so unlike the Keegan I met. I take a chance and crawl into his lap, laying my head on his chest. He wraps his arms around me, holding me tightly to him.

"This right here feels like home to me. You're my home, Bec." As much as his words warm my heart, it still breaks it when he calls me 'Bec.' I try to keep my voice from giving away the pain my heart is feeling right now. He needs me, I can feel it.

"Keegan, I'm not mad, I just wish I could remember what happened between us. That doesn't mean I wouldn't have done it without influence. I love you, Keegan, don't be upset because you think I regret sleeping with you last night." Before I can say anything, he's out from under me, leaning with his back to me against the wall. He

The Broken Girl

looks so distraught, I want to go to him but I feel it will only make things worse.

"Keegan. Please." I just need him to look at me.

"Bec, no just please give me a minute." Watching him suffer is tearing me apart. I watch him pace back and forth before sitting in a chair with his head in his hands.

"Bec, I need you to listen to me. Just let me say everything; let me get it all out. Because once I tell you everything you will hate me." With that, I'm up from the bed kneeling beside him. I pull his hands from his face and place my hand on his face. He leans in and lightly kisses my hand while bringing his over top of mine. The heat from the contact in my hand would bring me to me knees had I not already been there. "Bec, you were drugged last night."

I feel as if my world just crashed. I'm hoping the world will open up and swallow me. "How?" He just shakes his head at me. "I don't remember anything, Keegan." My breath begins to escape me. I am hyperventilating and losing control. My chest is pounding and a tight feeling has started closing in on my heart. "I can't breathe."

Keegan picks me up off the floor and carries me back to the bed. Being in this bed doesn't help, with what happened in this bed. "Out, I can't be in this bed." Keegan looks at me with hurt eyes, and I see tears pooling in them.

"You think we had sex while I knew you were drugged?" I'm shaking my head because I know he would never let that happen, if he knew what he's saying.

"Did someone…" I crack and I'm overcome with tears cascading down my face.

"No, Bec, you tried to get help. You found me but just as you did, you collapsed. No one… raped you. I was with you all night. You were asleep all night. I stayed awake until I knew you were in the clear."

The pain on his face is still evident, and I don't understand. "Why would I hate you for taking care of me? You saved me. What if I hadn't found you?" Looking into his eyes, he sits next to me on the bed. I see the tears he's tried so hard to keep at bay sliding down his cheeks.

"I asked myself that a million times last night. What if you didn't get to me? What if someone had done something to you?" Keegan is shattered.

"But it didn't. I was safe because of you."

The Broken Girl

"Don't thank me, Bec. The drugs where my fault." He won't look at me and I'm stunned.

Wait?

What? Is he telling me he did this to me?

"Keegan… are you telling me you drugged me, on purpose?" The fear that I may be in a room with someone who has done this to me begins to take hold of me. He says nothing. He just sits there. I get up from the bed and his head falls into his hands.

"KEEGAN! Are you saying that you, unbeknownst to me, gave me drugs?" I'm screaming now. Why would he do this to me? The tears are falling down my face at an alarming rate. If I weren't so angry I would be in the corner cowering. He gets up to come and try to comfort me. He goes to hug me and I start fighting him, screaming and pounding my fists on his chest.

"How could you? Keegan… I trusted you! Why? I love you, Keegan, but I will never forgive you for this. I can't even look at you. God. If you loved me you would never have done this to me. I don't even know who you are. Get out. I never want to see you again." He just holds me harder. I thought I knew him. Why would he do this to me?

"I won't make excuses. It's called a party favour. You are fine, but you are right. You shouldn't forgive me, Bec, I'm sorry I did this to you. I will never forgive myself for this, that I promise you." He brings his head down to my hair and squeezes me one last time before he walks out of the room, leaving me utterly broken.

Keegan drugged me.

Just like that, my entire world has turned on me. As I find the corner of the room and sink to the floor, the only thing that keeps going through my head is the one thing I will never know.

Why, Keegan?

***

Keegan

My insides feel like they are on fire. My heart is crashing against my ribs. I bring my hand up and wipe the tears that are falling. Crying isn't something I've done before. Not that I remember, anyway. This girl has destroyed the walls I've always kept up. I can hear her in the room bawling. All I keep hearing is her asking why. Why did I do this to her? God, I just want to run in there and

The Broken Girl

grab her. Kiss her and tell her I didn't know about it. That it was done to hurt us. But I can't. I won't be that selfish because, either way, it's still my fault she was drugged. When she said I couldn't love her if I did this to her, it was as if she jammed her hand inside my chest and ripped out her hand with my heart in her grasp.

I walk down the hall and I can't focus. All I feel is my heart being crushed. She will never see me again. She can't look at me. When she said those words, it was like she put a knife into my heart and twisted. I need an outlet, something to take the edge off before I run back in there. Without a thought, I spin and put my fist through the wall. As soon as I feel the pressure, it takes the pain away from my heart. I see my hand sitting inside the wall. Pulling it out, I see that my knuckles are bleeding. My fist is throbbing, but this sting doesn't last long before I'm reminded of the heartbreak. I'm heaving while trying to get a grip on my emotions.

"Keegan, you can't do this to her."

I turn around and come face to face with Charlotte. Her eyes are red and I know she's been crying. "Don't you dare, Charlotte. I can't do much for her but I can do this." She grabs me by the arm and brings me down the stairs and right out into the backyard. It's too early for anyone to be out, and I'm happy for the lack of company because Charlotte isn't going to go along with my plan easily.

"Keegan, why? I heard her. She will never get past this. I get it, you want to protect her, but she will hate you forever for this."

I turn away from her, blocking her from seeing the tears that are falling. "I want her to hate me. She should hate me. Sarah did this to get back at me. She wanted Bec to stay away from me. What if she didn't stop there? What if she tried again and we aren't so lucky that one of us found her?" Charlotte puts her hand on my shoulder. She is so much like her cousin.

"We should call the police. They will handle Sarah."

"No. We have no proof, but our word against hers. Bec doesn't remember anything. Sarah's brother is a hotshot lawyer in Ottawa. She's not stupid. She won't go down for this. Bec will be made to look like a foolish girl who had too much to drink and came up with a lie to get out of it. I won't let that be Bec, not because of me. I can't. Her parents will find out and she will be dragged back home and that will kill her. I won't be the reason for that. So I will take the hate, all of it." I am barely able to finish my sentence.

The Broken Girl

My entire body is betraying me. Trying to stay calm isn't working.

"Keegan, why would you do any of this? I can tell how much this is killing you."

"Because I love Bec, every goddamn broken piece of her." Those are the final words that bust up the gates holding me together. This girl has climbed inside and ripped me apart. I begin to bring myself down to the ground, putting my head in between my knees. Charlotte brings her arms around my shoulder and hugs me. "I know you do. I never doubted that. She may never know the extent you've gone for her and what you've given up. But I do, and I will never forget what you've done for my cousin, Keegan. Thank you for loving her for who she really is."

I can't respond because my words have escaped me. My heart is upstairs, not but a hundred feet away, thinking I drugged her. Wishing she'd never met me, hoping to never lay eyes on me again. Those thoughts are killing me. "She really is amazing, Charlotte. I will never stop loving her."

"Oh, Keegan, A broken man loving a broken girl."

Broken by me.

~ 138 ~

Chapter Sixteen

Becca

What the hell just happened?

"Why?" I keep repeating this. Keegan, oh my god.

"He drugged me." What the hell is a party favour? Seriously, am I supposed to be okay with this? Did he really expect that? Broken doesn't even begin to describe my heart right now. Keegan has hurt me in the past but this is a whole different level. I don't want to believe he would be capable of doing this to me but he said it himself. Maybe I don't know him at all. My Keegan is dead and gone. I hear a crash but I'm too emotionally drained to go check it out. Crawling across the floor, I pull myself into the chair in the corner and pull a blanket over me, trying to shut out the world.

I must have nodded off because I hear Charlotte. "Jake, now isn't the time, okay?" The door opens and I look over to see Jake

The Broken Girl

standing there. His eyes are tired and he clearly hasn't slept at all.

"Charlotte, no. I need to talk to her so either get out or stay." Charlotte looks to me with such pity. Has she talked to Keegan? Does everyone know?

"Becca, you don't have to do this right now." The look on her face is telling me to send Jake away but I just can't right now. I need him.

"Charlotte, shut the door. I need to see Jake." Jake's face is full of relief, however, Charlotte looks nervous. She does what I ask though.

"Call me if you need me, Becca. This will get better. I promise you." Well, that answers my question about her knowing about the drugs. She pulls the door closed quietly and leaves me with Jake.

"Jake." It's all I get out before my tears have returned.

"Becca, I am so sorry." I don't want to talk about any of this; I just need Jake right now. He's always there when I need him. "Becca, I need to talk to you. I just need you to listen okay." I'm shaking my head before he's finished.

"No. I've done enough listening today, I think."

~ 140 ~

"Becca, I need to clarify some things about what went down last night. Alec doesn't know." I was ready to stop him and scream for him to shut up but this is something I didn't know.

"Alec doesn't know about the drugs?" Jake shakes his head in response.

"We knew if he found out about it he'd have called an ambulance and your parents. I know you didn't want them to try and make you go home again." Jake was thinking about me. At least someone was worried about how this would screw up my life.

"When you say *we*?" I begin to ask him the question, but I feel like I already know the answer.

"Charlotte, Keegan, and myself." I gasp. Charlotte must have known afterwards. She'd never have let the drugs be given to me. I begin to back away from him, pulling myself up in the chair.

Jake is looking at me with such pain on his face. I'm so tired of everyone else feeling hurt. "You knew about the drugs and didn't stop it." Jake had been reaching out to put his hand on me. When he heard what I said, he pulled back as if I had stung him.

"You think I knew about the drugs before? You think I'd let that happen to you. I know you don't remember but we had a

The Broken Girl

fight last night. Even though I was angry, I'd never knowingly let harm come to you, Becca. I love you."

This is why I had always run to Jake. He was my rock, the one I could always depend on. "Wait, we fought? About what, Jacob?" He seems upset and I wonder how bad it was.

"None of it matters because I was so stupid to do it." He's trying to brush what happened under the rug, so I must have been awful to him.

"Jake, please tell me. I feel like everything has been taken from me. I want to know." The irony of how Keegan must be feeling with his memory loss isn't lost on me, but I push him out of my mind.

My hand goes to lie over top of Jake's and rub the top of his hand with the bottom of my thumb. "I told you goodbye." The hand that had been resting on Jake's is now no longer there. It was as if it automatically recoiled at his words.

"You did it again. You pushed me away, Jake."

"Becca, God, I was so stupid. I regret it so much." He looks torn but I can't begin to understand. I'm too emotionally overwhelmed.

"Jake, just go. I don't need your pity. It's become very clear to me that I'm very much on my own here. After everything we've been through, you were just going to walk away. I don't need people like that in my life, Jacob." He goes tense at my use of his name. He begins looking around as if the room has the answers he is so desperately seeking.

"Keegan…"

I interrupt him. "Jake, I don't want to talk about Keegan, not now, not ever. I'm done with him." My tone was firm. He looks lost at my words but doesn't question it.

"Sarah…"

I put my hands up stopping him again. "I definitely don't want to talk about that stupid bitch either." He lets out a heavy sigh.

"Fine, Becca. Just know I'm sorry. I didn't mean to hurt you. You're my best friend." I pull Jake to me and wrap my arms around him. Jake is safe. He always has been. "Becca, no one will ever know what happened, I promise you." I hold him tightly pressing him against me. "But Becca, there is something I have to tell you about last night and I need to tell you. I need you to just listen, please. I'm begging you to just remember I love you."

My heart drops. I feel like the rug is again about to be pulled out from under me.

The Broken Girl

I just nod because I know I won't be able to use my words. "Becca, before our fight is when I'm assuming the drug mishap happened. Then we had this huge blowout and I said some awful things, which I'm glad you don't remember. There was just so much anger. I didn't want to fight any more after you walked away from me." My heart slowly starts coming back to its rightful place. If a big fight is all I need to worry about, I can deal with that, especially in light of all the chaos that has taken over my life.

"Jake, I don't blame you for not wanting to fight with me. I walked away most likely so no further damage could be done." I'm not sure if that's true or if I walked away because the damage was already done, but I guess I will never know. There seem to be a lot of unanswered questions lately.

"Becca, you walked away because I told you I was done, that I was letting go."

I can't move. I just sit there. I know he'd said this already, but to hear him tell me why he hadn't chased me was a whole different thing.

"Okay." That's all I can say. I don't really know what he expects me to say but this can't be the entire bomb he's looking to drop on me. "Jake, I don't remember the fight, so can't we just leave it at that? Unless you'd like to reiterate it so I know what you actually want from me." The sarcasm in my voice is definitely being picked up on by Jake now.

"Becca, something happened before Keegan found you." I wince at his name and the facts of him 'saving me.'

"What, Jake, is it really important? I already know this is entirely his fault. Can't we just leave it at that and move on." Did something happen to me that Keegan didn't know about? "I don't want to know. If something happened to me I'd rather be ignorant to it, thank you very much."

"God, Beckers, no! Nothing like that happened to you. I promise." Now I'm lost. What is he talking about?

"Jakey, you're worrying me now."

"Just know that I love you. I never would have done this had I known. I should have known just by the sound of your voice, but I was too hurt to pay any attention." His words are like ice in my veins.

"What did you do, Jacob?" My mind is running away with ideas of what happened last night. Did I catch him with someone again? Was it Kristy? Did he tell me he didn't love me?

"After you ran away from me, you were gone for about twenty minutes. You came

The Broken Girl

behind me and called my name. I should have known, but I didn't. I just walked away from you, Becca. I left you drugged and alone." And just like that everything I thought I knew about the people in my life had changed.

I move away from him, putting some much needed distance between us. "Did you look at me, Jake? Did you see me when I spoke your name?"

He shakes his head. "You were behind me, and I heard you call my name. I never turned around, I just walked out the door and left."

"You were that mad at me that you couldn't even look at me. You couldn't just say anything to me. What the hell is wrong with you people?" I will not cry any more today, or so my mind tells my tears, but they don't seem to be listening.

"Becca, if I had known..."

"No! But you didn't because you were too upset with me, right? Too upset to turn and even glance at your best friend." Jake's eyes are glazed over and I know he's hurting, but I'm enraged.

"Leave."

"Becca, no, please." He goes to reach for me but I pull away. "I said leave! Come on, Jake, you should be good at it by now.

You wanted to leave me last night so just do it. Leave, I don't need a friend who left me alone when I needed him. I run to you Jake, I always have and when I needed you... Where were you? Fucking Kristy again?" He winces at my tone and words. I know I'm being harsh but I don't give a shit. The two people I thought I could trust have let me down.

"I'm sorry my life is screwed up and I couldn't just deal with it normally. This isn't easy for me, and nothing has been clear to me until now. The confusion and doubts I had have left. I choose... and it's neither of you. I choose heartbreak. That's what you've done to me, Jacob Kelso. As much as I love Keegan, it was always you I went to... Why? Because you were the love of my life." All the tears have dried up. I feel like this is it for everything. I'm done.

"I love you, Rebecca. Believe that." Jake is just staring at me, trying to reach into my heart, but my heart is in a million pieces right now and is in no way ready to be put back together. "Damn it, Becca, why can't you just let me love you, for fuck sakes. I love you. Why is that so wrong? Why do you push me away?"

Really. I'm pushing him away. "No, Jake, you pushed me away. You pushed me to stay with Keegan. You left me alone in

The Broken Girl

the dorms and you told me goodbye yesterday."

"You don't understand, Becca. Just let me love you." Jake is pleading with his eyes but my heart isn't responding. It's using the only strength it has left to keep it beating.

"That's not an option anymore, Jacob. You know why? Because on a scale of one to a million, I'm a million percent fucked up, that's why. Whose fault is that, I wonder? Jacob, I want you to leave. It shouldn't be too hard, you were ready to do it twelve hours ago." The inner bitch has reared her head and I don't see her going away anytime soon.

"Jake, you need to go." I turn to see my brother standing in the doorframe, confused at the scene before him. "I don't know what the hell your problem is, Jake. I didn't hear much but what I heard I didn't like. She asked you to leave. Now I'm telling you to get the hell away from her."

"Alec, it's a misunderstanding. I swear." Alec shakes his head and points to get out. Jake walks up to my brother and I'm worried it's going to get physical.

"Stay away from my sister until you get your shit straight." Jake let the tenseness leave his shoulders. "I love her, man, you know that. If she needs a friend to talk to or anything, I'm here for her no matter what you say about it. I will always be there for her."

Alec lets out a sarcastic laugh. "Not from what I've heard. I hear you threw a pussy fit when she didn't run off into the sunset with you. She had doubts; she's allowed a moment to have some fucking doubts. For fuck sake, her whole damn world came crashing down around her. Don't act like Key. She deserves a good guy and if that can't be you, or you keep fucking up, I will make damn sure she is never around you, friendly or not. I will push her towards anyone but you. Now leave her alone until she comes to you. Maybe you will be lucky and she will. But you don't deserve a damn thing from where I'm standing. You and Key are both screwed."

Jake turns and looks at me. "Becca, you might not believe me, but I love you. I think I was right last night." I know what's coming so for self-preservation, so I do it first.

"Love can be toxic if given to you by the wrong person. Some use it as a weapon and others use it in desperation. I know how I love you, but clearly I'm alone in that since you're trying to give me a goodbye speech again. Just get the fuck out of here, Jake. You got what you wanted. Goodbye."

The Broken Girl

"Becca, I missed the hell outta you." Jake uses our words to try and salvage this conversation, but the damage is done.

"Goodbye, Jake."

Jake is speechless, and he just turns and storms out. I didn't mean what I said about his love being toxic or any of it, but I won't be this pathetic girl that everyone keeps dumping.

"Becca, what happened?" Yeah, I'm not going there, not now, not ever.

"Your sister's love life just exploded, but hey, what else is new?" I'm pushing myself to keep being snarky in order to keep my emotions in check.

"Becca, it's okay. I know what that took for you to say." Oh, Alec, if you only really knew.

"I don't want to feel like this anymore." If Jake doesn't want me, and the Keegan I love is gone, then why bother. If they are both like this, I'm better off lonely and broken.

Chapter Seventeen

It's been two weeks. I haven't so much as talked to Jake or Keegan. They have kept their distance, which I think hurts more. I know I said to stay away, but I thought they would try at least. Instead I see them laughing and talking with friends as if they didn't just break me into a million tiny shards. They've looked at me but I always turn and look away. Alec eventually dropped the questions and gave up. It's not hard to believe that my love life is really that screwed up. He didn't like that I wouldn't hang out with him and his friends anymore. I made a joke about dating another one of them and he dropped it. Telling him it is time I live away from them all and get my own friends was really freeing.

It was the most heart-shattering thing I've ever done. Not knowing what is going on in Jake and Keegan's life is unbearable, but there is just too much damage done. Meeting girls from the dorm was awesome. They were all about having fun, but keeping out of trouble. Until tonight, which I knew if my brother or Charlotte knew about, they'd be pissed.

Standing in front of my mirror, I feel like I'm not Bec or Becca anymore. For tonight, I'm not. I'm Larissa Cole. At least that's what my fake ID says. The girls thought it would be fun to play dress-up with Becca. I'm wearing six inch silver stilettos and a red short dress that I swear is cutting my breathing off.

"Damn girl, where were you hiding that body of yours?" I turn and see Nicky standing at the door. She is taller than me and curvy in all the right sort of places. Her hair is jet black and curly.

"I don't know, maybe I just didn't have a reason to flaunt it." I am trying to be the new confident, Becca.

"No, you had no reason to get all dolled up with those boys from the team chasing you, but tonight it's all about new prospects." Lily has arrived at my door as well. She has chestnut brown hair with blonde streaks and has a body a runway model would kill for. She also doesn't work for it. She eats more than any girl I have ever seen and just spouts some crap about a great metabolism.

Gracie Wilson

"Come on, bitch. It's game time." They say in unison. I laugh at them. "Let's go, bitches."

When we arrive at the club, my confidence has gone down. Lilly seems to pick up on it. "Don't worry, we will get right in and get you some liquid courage." We walk up to the bouncer who takes our IDs. He barely looks at them. Instead he is just looking at us in our outfits and nods us in.

"He only takes the IDs to check them to cover his ass. He'd let us in if it was my grandma's ID." Nicky is all about the truth. She doesn't sugar coat anything, which I find pretty awesome. Looking around the club, it's not what I've expected. It doesn't seem to have endless possibilities. Really, it is just four walls with some fancy lights and a DJ. I hear a familiar laugh and I don't have to turn around to know it's Jake.

"Drink time," I say to the girls and they cheer, hauling me off to the side bar.

"What can I get you ladies?" The bartender asks what we'd like; I don't wait for the girls to answer before I order. "Nine shots of Tequila." I hand him money and he starts pouring our shots. I take the first one and down it.

"Come on now, don't make me do them alone." Nicky just laughs while Lily is

The Broken Girl

shaking her head. Nicky grabs one and down it goes like nothing.

"Lily doesn't do tequila." I look to Lily hoping for some explanation.

"Tequila makes my clothes come off and it's too early for that shit." I laugh and grab my other two shots and down they go. It burns but I'm using this to keep my mind off the group behind us. I don't want to think about Jake or Keegan tonight, that was the deal. Nicky grabs her two and downs them; I look to Lily and smile.

"Last chance." She shakes her head, laughing. "More for me," I say, then drink the last two shots.

"Dance time!" I cheer. They both giggle and agreed. Not before we each have another drink to take with us though. I'm not even sure what mine is but it's fruity and yummy. I make my way into the middle of the dance floor, making sure I'm covered so Jake won't see me. Not that I'd care if he said something. I just don't want him to make me leave. Tonight is about my fun and having it my way.

The music is pounding through the speakers and the bass makes the floor vibrate up through my shoes. A few guys have come up to me but I just wasn't into it and told them I was out with the girls

Gracie Wilson

tonight. The lights are spinning and I'm feeling great. I'm not tanked but I have an awesome buzz going on. My drink needs to be filled again so I take off to the bar, leaving the girls on the dance floor with guys flocking towards them. I laugh as I walk away.

As I approach the bar, I don't even think about where I am. I'm all about the fun right now. The bartender gives me the same thing I've been getting all night, which I found out is called a jolly rancher. I decide to hang out at the bar for a bit before returning to the maze on the dance floor.

"Hey, what's your name and can I buy you a drink?" He sounds cocky. I turn around to find Jake and Keegan standing next to this guy who I have seen around. I know he plays hockey with them. Keegan and Jake's backs are turned to me so they don't see who he's talking to. "Wait a minute… aren't you Potts' sister?" With that, both Keegan and Jake spin around to find me standing here trapped.

Before they even get a word out, I turn to the bartender. "Two shots of tequila." He pours them for me and I down them. I don't even feel the burning anymore. I turn to leave but Keegan and Jake are standing in my way. "What are you doing here, Becca?" Jake says.

The Broken Girl

"It's neither of your business what I do or where I go. Now, if you will excuse me. My new friends who aren't interested in fucking with my heart are dancing and I'm going to join them." I go to step around them and they both get in my way, causing me to bump into a guy I recognize as the teacher's assistant for Charlotte's English class.

"You're not going anywhere, but out that door with us, Bec," Keegan says. "He's right. Fun time is over, Becca," Jake adds.

"I don't believe I'd asked for your permission." I go to leave and I notice that the guy I bumped into is watching me. So I get brave and spiteful.

"Hey, do you happen to play hockey?" He looks puzzled.

"No."

I smile. "Well, if the way you're looking at me is any indication of interest, how about we dance?" He smirks at me and takes my hand, guiding me out to the dance floor. We end up next to Lily and Nicky who give me the thumbs-up.

"I'm Tracey," he says.

"Becca," I add. He smiles and puts his hands on my waist moving against me to the music. After a few songs I've somehow loosened up and am now turned around with my backside grinding into his front. I look up, seeing Keegan and Jake staring at me. Jake is on the phone and he doesn't look happy. Great, they are probably calling my brother or Charlotte.

I'd forgotten I was dancing with Tracey until his lips graze my neck. I see Keegan and Jake glare this way and I know it won't be long before they start over here. I motion for Lily and Nicky to come to me and they do.

"See those two guys? Those are my old boyfriends. Distract them so I can get out of here." They nod and Nicky gives me a wink.

I turn to Tracey. "Want to get out of here?" His face lights up as if he just won the jackpot. I'm not really sure what I meant by what I said. At this point, I can't screw things up any more. Linking arms with Tracey, I maneuver us out the side entrance and he waves down a cab. We quickly get in and set off. I'm assuming it is towards his place.

As soon as we pull up, his lips are on me. I don't even get a chance to take in my surroundings, but instead of doing the Becca thing and over think things. I say screw it. I give him everything I have, causing him to gasp at my willingness. I am always trying to do everything right in my life, so maybe it's time to try something wrong. We

The Broken Girl

somehow make it inside of his building and he fumbles with his keys. As soon as his door is open, we are inside. His mouth hasn't left mine. I want to say it's hot and amazing but it nothing compared to my more recent kisses.

I hear the door shut behind us and before I know it, we are crashing into his bed. His shirt is gone and I feel his skin against me. He brings his hands up my back, undoing the zipper of my dress. It slides off easy, exposing the black Victoria's Secret set Charlotte had told me was to die for. He seems to agree because I hear his belt buckle undo and his pants are now off. All that's left is his boxers. I try to pace things but his hands are all over me. He's just about to slip his hands into my panties when I hear a noise. "Get the hell off of her right now."

Tracey jumps back, leaving me exposed on the bed. I rush to wrap his blanket around me. Alec and Drake are staring at me. "Oh shit." I say.

"Yeah, Becca. Oh shit is right. Time to go." I shake my head, not really wanting to stay, but definitely not wanting to deal with my severely pissed off brother.

"Alec, no. Drake, take him home." Drake shakes his head at me and I know I'm all alone in this one.

"I don't know what's going on here but it isn't anything she didn't want. It was her idea to leave the club." Ugh, thanks, Tracey. I could have lived without my brother knowing that.

"That is my sister and she's leaving," Alec says.

"She looks grown up enough to me to make her own choices and I don't think Becca wants to leave." Oh, this guy is going to end up getting his ass kicked.

"Did my very grown up sister also tell you she is only eighteen?" Tracey turns to me, looking shocked, and I just shrug.

"I didn't know, but it's still not a big deal. She's still an adult. She's hot and I'm not making her leave."

"We aren't asking buddy. Becca, Alec will either walk out of here with you or he will drag your drunk ass out of here," Drake replies.

"Seriously, you both are killing my buzz. Fine, clearly next time I have to go out of town if I want to get any." I throw the blankets off me and grab my dress, slipping it back on and zipping it up. Grabbing my shoes, I just glare at Alec and Drake. I turn and walk up to Tracey and kiss him. He responds and I hear my brother growl.

"Now, Becca," Drake says.

The Broken Girl

"Thanks for some fun, Tracey." I smirk at him before stalking out of the apartment.

It isn't until I am walking out the front that I realize this is Keegan's apartment building. Once I clear the bushes I see Keegan and Jake standing there waiting.

"Thanks for ratting me out. Clearly unless I'm screwing one of you, you can't keep your damn mouths shut." I know it's the alcohol talking, but I don't care at this point. I don't stop and continue walking right across the street to my brother's house. Charlotte is standing at the door wide eyed.

"Yeah, I'm not doing this right now, Charlotte."

She just laughs and shakes her head at me. "Becca, I don't have to say anything. You are going to have one hell of a hangover tomorrow."

I laugh. "Hey, I'm okay with that. I had some free no strings fun tonight. Can't beat that, can you?

"Really, so that's who you are now?" I turn and see that Keegan and Jake have followed me back here with Alec and Drake.

"You both destroyed me. You don't get to judge me on how I put myself back together. It doesn't matter who I am, Jake. I am an adult and will do what I want." He just shakes his head.

"Yeah, I saw that tonight. How'd it feel with some random guy taking you home?"

I feel as though he slapped me. "A lot better than when my best friend broke my heart."

"Guys, let's not do this right now," Drake says.

"Just everyone cool down." Alec shakes his head. "Man, I'm done being a referee. Maybe what they need is a good fight where no one is afraid to say the wrong thing." Oddly, my brother makes sense or it may just be the tequila.

"Bec, what the hell where you thinking? Getting drunk like that and then going home with Tracey?" I'm shocked that he knows his name, only making this slightly embarrassing to my drunken brain.

"I wanted to have some fun… you know what that's like right, Key? At least I stayed out of the party favours." Keegan looks hurt and nervous but I don't stop. "What I do and who I do it with is no one's business but my own. Got it?"

Jake is just shaking his head. "The hell it is, Becca. You can't just screw around because you want to or because you want to get back at us."

Who the hell does he think he is? "My screwing had nothing to do with you two.

The Broken Girl

Unbeknownst to you two, my love life or sexual life doesn't revolve around you."

"Apparently it revolves around whatever guy gives you attention." Keegan says.

"Really let's not talk about attention seekers right now. Why don't you go fuck Sarah some more? She's always looking for some screwing around isn't she... or wait, better yet, why don't you fuck me and call me her name again cause that was one hell of a time."

Keegan's face goes bright red. "I'm done with this shit. I'm leaving."

He goes to walk out and I yell at him. "At least this time you're leaving me awake, better than last time isn't it, Keegan." He stops for a second but then continues out the door.

"What the hell was that about, Becca?" Alec asks.

"Nope, I'm not talking about it some things in my life are not your business." I'm not drunk enough for this conversation.

"The hell it isn't." Alec replies.

"God, Alec, you're fucking with my buzz. Just stop, okay? For once I wasn't trying to screw one of your friends, so be happy about that." Alec winces and I know I went too far, not only throwing Keegan and Jake in his face, but Michael too.

"Guys, let me talk to Becca for a minute," Jake says.

I look to Drake, Alec, and Charlotte, hoping for some help but they don't look impressed enough right now to save me from this awkwardness. They all leave and head to the basement.

"I'm leaving," I say.

"No, you're not leaving until you talk to me, Beckers."

I snap. "Don't call me that any more, Jake. I'm nothing. Remember you said goodbye? You don't get to be all 'Beckers' now."

"I lied to you, Becca."

Whoa, what?

He sees my confusion and continues. "I was an idiot and I didn't want to lose you so I ended it first. I pushed and pushed because I figured you'd go back to Keegan and I'd be without you."

My heart stops. "You did what?" I ask.

"Sending you away was because I didn't want to let you in and then lose you. It's enough losing you as my best friend, but losing you, and not having all of you? That's just too much."

Jake wants to be with me or he had wanted to. "Becca, I did something I regret."

The Broken Girl

My heart jumps up to my throat. "What did you do, Jake?"

Seeing his eyes, I know this is going to crush me. "I slept with someone. I'd been drinking and she was there. It didn't mean anything." With that, any of the warm feeling I was having for Jake vanished.

"Well, go do some more things that don't mean anything. If I meant anything to you that wouldn't have happened!"

Jake's face turns rigid and I can see him getting angry. "So, wait. You tell Keegan you can do what you want, but we can't?" I know he has a point but my heart and brain aren't connected.

I scream. "I only hooked up tonight because you broke my fucking heart Jake. You said goodbye not one but three times. I may not remember one of them but, trust me, the two I remember did enough damage. Now you say you did it to protect your heart. Well dumb fucking move. My heart was always yours, but now it never will be."

"Charlotte!" I scream. She comes running up the stairs. "I'm leaving and I'm not sleeping here. I doubt I'm going to be 'allowed' to leave alone. So either come with me or tie me down because that's the only two options you have.

"Okay, let's get you out of here." Thank god for Charlotte and knowing what I really need.

We grab her bag, leaving with Jake just standing with his mouth wide open in shock.

"Now it's my turn to say goodbye, Jake."

The Broken Girl

Chapter Eighteen

Jake hasn't stopped calling my phone or texting me. They are all apologies. I only sent one message back. Telling him I just needed some space. What I wanted to say was goodbye but my heart just couldn't do it. He never wrote me after that message today. Jake is hurting, and I get that pain. No need to add salt to the wound. Keegan hasn't so much as looked at me. Sarah and him are close again. That's about all I noticed and it made my stomach turn. They deserve each other. Charlotte never said anything about what happened. I never talked about it with Nicky and Lily. To top it off it's exam time so I'm studying and have no social life. Not that I could even handle one right now. I was working in the library most the time but Jake always seemed to be there. I've now started hiding in my dorm, studying. Over-studying is a true fact. I feel like I may be bordering that right now, but with my mind in a book I don't have the energy to feel everything from the last few weeks.

There is a knock at my door and I take my time getting up. It's either Drake or Charlotte. They have been 'popping' in to check on me. Charlotte hasn't told Drake yet, but we have talked about it. I am going to leave. My art program for the summer starts right after exams finish and I'm ready to get out of here for a while. When I open my door, all thoughts leave my head.

"Please don't shut the door." Standing in front of me is a dishevelled Jake. His hair is a mess but still very Jake and sexy. But something about him is off. He's not confident or vibrant. He looks like he hasn't slept in days.

"Jake? Are you okay?" I ask because something isn't right here. This isn't the Jake I know.

"No, Becca, I'm not okay. I haven't been okay and I don't think I will be again." Jake has always been honest and upfront but seeing him so bare makes me raw.

"Jake," I sigh.

"No. I need you to listen. You're the last thing I think about every night. You're everything I need. When I walked away, I just wanted you to be happy." I go to say something but he puts his fingers to my lips, hushing me.

The Broken Girl

"You asked for space. I can give you anything but that. I know what you want. Becca, I tried. God, I tried. But I can't just forget you. Every single minute, the pain of not having you in my life eats at me. All of the things I'm doing and saying don't change how empty I feel without you. I know you hate me and don't love me. But baby, I need you." Jake is holding himself up with the doorframe; it looks like it's the only thing keeping him standing.

"Jake, we can't keep doing this to each other. Look at you; this isn't how it's supposed to be. It isn't supposed to be this hard," I say, trying to keep my emotions in check.

"I'm here to say I'm sorry. I know how bad I messed things up. God, you're everything. I let you down in the worst way. It twisted me up inside every single fucking day, Becca." His head is hanging and I know he feels defeated.

"Becca, I pushed you away because having you, all of you, then losing you would destroy my heart forever. You're the first face that I see. You're the reason I am alive. You're all I see, you're my future." I bring my hand to his chest and put it gently against his heart.

"Jacob…" He doesn't move.

He interrupts me. "Don't make me be alone, because loving you is as good as it gets. My life can never get better than that. When it's said and done, Becca, you're my only way. The only thing that has every made sense to me, don't you see it? I won't go; walking away again isn't going to happen. I will never sleep, not until you're with me again and in my arms where you belong. I will never leave you; you're it for me."

I can tell he's trying to keep his breathing in check. He's trying to look away from me so I don't see the tears in his eyes that have begun to fall. I reach up to him and press my lips softly against his wet lips. I can feel the tears on his face against mine. "That's how we need to end things."

I turn away from him because I can't look at him right now. My heart is on, begging me to just let go and let Jake in.

"Becca." His voice is raspy and he is breathing heavily.

"Jake, I still love you."

Before I know it, I am being spun around and am in his arms. His lips crash down on mine and I forget how much he hurt me. How much I'm hurting over Keegan. It's Jake. I moan and he takes this opportunity to deepen our kiss. His tongue slips in and I feel his hands grabbing me

The Broken Girl

tighter. He pushes me back and shuts the door, locking it. I feel his hand graze the hem of my shirt and every spot he touches causes heat at the contact.

"Jake," I say hesitantly. We shouldn't be doing this. Everything is so messed up. "Please just let me touch you." His words are my undoing.

I let go.

My hands find their way into his hair and his hands move, holding my head in place. The kiss is filled with so many things. I can almost taste the desperation coming from him. He's trying to tell me something, but I don't know what it is.

"Becca. Baby," he says, against my lips and he then continues his mouth along my jaw. He begins working down my neck. Each time he moves, there is a trail of tingling left behind. My body is on hypersensitive.

I back up to my bed, pulling Jake with me. Grabbing his shirt, I pull it over his head, only breaking apart when I had to. Jake is watching me, taking the cues from me. My hands slide down his chest and I feel him tense at the contact. *Don't stop this, Jake.* Looking into his eyes, I bring my mouth to his chest just where his heart is and I kiss the spot softly. Never breaking eye contact. I hear Jake groan and this makes my body ache.

He isn't taking this further; he's just content with what we are doing now. The sweetness is not lost on me but my body is craving more. I start pulling off my shirt and I feel him gasp. My shirt is off, leaving me in my jeans and a pale pink lace bra.

"Becca…" Jake is struggling, but I need this. We need this.

"Please don't stop, Jakey. I want you to touch me, feel me. You say you need me, but that's nothing to how much I need you." All the reservations he had leave him and he pulls me to him, colliding my mouth with his. His hand slides down my backside and sweep around to the front undoing my button of my jean slowly. He's giving me a chance to stop him but that won't be happening.

"I love you, Jake." My voice is raspy. "It's you, baby, it's always been you." His words seal my choice. He slowly slides my jeans down and I step out of them leaving me in just my bra and undies. His fingers trail along my hipbone causing shivers to run through my body. Looking into Jake's eyes, I see only love and affection. It's everything I'd been hoping to see. Sliding my hands from his chest, I start undoing his belt followed by the button and zipper to his

The Broken Girl

jeans. His breathing is heavy, causing my body to respond the same way. When I bring my eyes back to his I see desire but a hint of hesitation is there. My hands begin to push his jeans down but his hands go over mine stopping me. "Becca…" I know what's coming.

"Jake, please?" He just looks at me. "Love me… I'm letting you love me, Jake. I'm yours." All hesitation leaves his eyes and he grabs my bottom, bringing me right against him. His eyes are glossy; there are so many emotions in them. "Make love to me, Jake. I love you. I'm ready."

I continue pulling his pants off him and he just watches me closely looking for any hint that I'm unsure. Finding the words to tell him how much I want this, I want him. Words aren't going to be enough. I bring my hands behind my back, undoing my bra. Slowly I slip my panties down my legs, never looking at Jake. I back up until I'm against my bed, I bring myself up onto it so I am sitting completely naked and exposed, but I don't hide. Bringing my eyes back to his, I slip my finger into the top of his boxers and pull him towards me. "Let me love you Jake."

He is now hovering over me; he hasn't taken his boxers off so I do it for him. When he sees this, he doesn't stop me, he just watches.

"I missed the ever loving hell out of you too, Jake." Just like that, he's on top of me. He's kissing me, sliding his hands against my flesh, leaving me craving more.

"I've been waiting to hear those words for too long, Becca." He holds himself over me, not putting his whole weight on me. I feel him harden against me and I thought I would feel embarrassed or unsure, but it only makes me want him more. Bringing my hands around his waist, I grab him and pull him towards me.

"I see you." Jake looks confused at my words. "You told me I'm your future… I see you… you are what I see in my future, Jacob Kelso."

"I love you, Becca." He is right at my opening and I push myself towards him, hinting at what I want. I feel him push slowly, filling me entirely. It is a shock at first, but I welcome the feeling. He slowly starts a pace and his hands graze my breasts, causing me to let out a moan.

"Jake." He picks up his pace but never do his eyes leave mine.

"Are you okay?"

I can't speak. I'm afraid if I open my mouth I will only moan louder. I nod and bring my mouth to his. He doesn't slow

The Broken Girl

down. He keeps going and I feel the desire in me filling. I lightly bite his bottom lip, causing him to groan in pleasure at me. Taking the opportunity, I massage his tongue with mine causing me to feel like I'm ready to fall off the edge.

"Jake." I plead.

"I know, baby. I'm right there with you." I feel my body tightening. This is new. I've never felt this before. He is moving faster now and I feel him panting against my shoulder. My body gives in to overwhelming sensations, falling over the edge, causing ever nerve to hum in pleasure.

"Becca." Jake is right there with me as we climax together.

We don't move. We just stay like this, holding each other.

"Becca." He brings his hand over my scar from where Dillon had slashed me with the knife. All those memories coming rushing back. The pain I caused Jake. I don't deserve to be this happy right now. I roll away from Jake.

"Becca, what's wrong?" I feel tears trying to break free and I just shake my head. "What is it?"

"Jake, I don't deserve this. All I've done is hurt those who love me." I bring my hand over my scar and Jake rolls me back into him. He looks down at my hand covering my scar.

"Becca, look." He brings my hand to where he had been stabbed and I feel every emotion of that horrible night come back. "Don't be sad. I'm not. You saved me that night."

I shake my head wanting to say all the things I'd said to him before about it being my fault, but instead something else comes out. "We saved each other."

He brings my hand to his mouth and kisses it softly. "Exactly." He slowly slides his mouth down my neck, stopping every little bit to give a small kiss. He continues until he is over my scar at my hip. "Beautiful. You're so damn beautiful, Becca." Just like that, we make love for the second time.

We could have been like this forever. Cuddling together in my bed the way it was always meant to be, with nothing between us. I would have been okay with that, but a knock comes to my door. Panicking, I get up, wrapping myself in a blanket.

"Darn, it's Charlotte. She was going to stop by." I go to the door and laugh at the fact that Jake and I just got caught. "There will be no way of talking myself out of this one." Jake laughs and I open the door.

"Keegan."

Chapter Nineteen

Keegan

Why did I come here? To be honest, I don't have the slightest clue what I'm doing. I just couldn't take the hate any more. I wanted to apologize for going off on her. Drinking was done that night and I wasn't pleased that she went home with some guy. I just need to see her. I can't explain it but it's a need.

I knock on the door of her dorm room and I hear movement inside before I hear laughing. Bec opens the door, laughing, in nothing but a blanket. Jake is behind her on the bed. Her mouth drops open and I am frozen. I'm too late.

"Keegan." Her voice still tugs at me but I'm too angry to think straight. Damn it, I was too late, and now she's with Jake. For some reason this all seems so familiar.

I shake away those thoughts and look into the eyes of the girl I love. She looked happy up until she saw who it was. "Screw this."

I go to leave but she puts her hand on my arm, causing me to still. "Keegan, I'm so sorry that you had to see this. I would never have wanted that." My heart knows that as much as she hates me, she would never cause me harm. That's my job.

"Key, man, I'd tell you it's not what it looks like, but well… it is." Yeah, thanks for the confirmation on that one, Jake.

"Keegan, what are you doing here?" That's a great question.

"I needed to see you. I know you hate me for what happened but I just needed to see you." Her face tells me that she isn't upset by what I say but she also isn't happy either.

"Why, Keegan?" Her eyes look to Jake who is just watching us. Might as well tell the truth.

"I miss you. I love you, Bec." She gasps, bringing her hand to her mouth and Jake just stands there silently. I'd be pissed if he was pulling this shit but he seems to just be letting me set the pace.

"You always hurt the ones you love," Bec says. I don't think she is necessarily talking to me but I know she means that I've hurt her.

The Broken Girl

"Keegan, the drugs…I can't look past that. I'm sorry, you took away my choices. You put me in danger. I can't be around someone like that." I mentally kick myself in the ass at bringing this up.

Jake looks at me like he's confused. "Becca what are you talking about?" Jake is talking to Bec and I freeze.

"Jake, I really don't want to do this again." She gives him a look that I hope will tell him to stop but he just glares at me.

"Jake, let it go," I say.

"Wait a minute. Becca, what do you think happened with the drugs?" My anger is boiling and he's going to screw it all up.

"Jake, shut up."

Bec looks torn. She doesn't know what's happening and I'd feel for her if I weren't so desperate to keep it from her.

"Becca, what do you think Keegan did?" Jake asks.

"Jake, are you really going to make me say it?" He nods at her and she sighs. "Keegan drugged me. Are you happy I said it?"

Just like that, the lights go on in Jake's head. I shake my head trying to get him to keep quiet. "Hell, no, you're not pulling this shit, Key," Jake says.

"You won, so just leave it be." I respond. "I don't want to win because Becca doesn't know the truth. Either you tell her or I will."

Bec is looking at us and I see the fear on her face. I say nothing. "What is going on?" she whispers.

"Fine, I will tell her then. Becca, Keegan didn't drug you." With that, everything I was doing to protect her went up in flames.

Bec's eyes find me and I see that she is confused. "Is it true?" she asks.

I don't respond. I'm worried if I open my mouth, she would hear how much seeing her like this is affecting me.

Jake grabs his pants and shuffles them back on. "Becca, you need to talk to Keegan and get all the facts."

I see the panic raise in her. I wish I could comfort her but I don't see anything other than more pain coming from my disclosures.

"Jake...?" she begs.

He puts his hand just over her hip. "Beautiful, remember." She gives him a small smile and I realize I'm not meant to understand what's going on. "I'll be next door in my dorm. Try and not be an ass, Key."

The Broken Girl

Jake leaves and Becca lets me into the room. She is still wrapped in a blanket. "I feel like this is going to take longer than I'd like to be wrapped up for. Turn around and shut the door so I can get into pajamas."

I do as she says, still not talking. Once the door is locked and my back is to her, I hear her shuffle around. The back of her door has a small metal mirror on it and I can see her naked back in the reflection. I try not to look but I can't seem to stop myself. I see her shirt slide down her and I look down to stop myself from getting worked up. That's not why I'm here, but I have to remind myself that.

"You can turn around now." Doing as she says, I turn to find her in pajamas. I really wish she were back in the blanket right now. "So…" Bec says, and I forgot that I was supposed to be telling her something. "Keegan, I want the truth, so don't make me get it from someone else. I think you owe me that." God, I owe her so much more than she will ever know. I tried the lying thing and all it did was eat at me. Hopefully the truth will come out and be the lesser of two evils.

"It was Sarah. She did this to you." I can't look at her so I am looking at her feet that are in some fuzzy pink puppy slippers.

"Why would Sarah do that to me? Did you know she was doing this?" she asks.

Here goes nothing. "No, I didn't know about it. Not until it was too late. Why… well, she said she wanted you to loosen up and that she was tired of me looking at you. She just wanted you to not be around me and me being focused on you. The main thing was to get you out of the way. I would have stopped this if I had known. I promise you, Bec."

I hear her let out a sigh. "I was having such a hard time believing you would intentionally hurt me like that. My heart just wasn't buying it but you told me flat out that it was you. Why would you cover for her?" she asks.

I look everywhere around the room, but directly at her. "Bec, I thought if you thought it was me you would hate me forever. That she would have no reason to try something like this again. I was protecting you." By the end of that, my voice was cracking.

"Oh, Keegan, I'm so sorry that I believed you when you said it. I should have known you'd never do that to me. At least now you know what she's capable of. God, I have so much to think about. Yes, I slept with Jake, but that doesn't mean that I don't care about you. I thought you were hurting

The Broken Girl

me." Poor Bec she doesn't know the half of it.

"Bec, I have something to tell you. But first I just need you to listen. Okay, babe?" I see the uncertainty in her eyes but she nods.

"I love you, Bec, and love when you say it to me. I need you to know that I love you more. You opened me up. I don't know what changed me and turned me into the person you fell in love with. But I do know that you have just cracked me open, leaving me raw. But in the most amazing way, you broke down all my walls. I hope you still feel that way about me."

She nods but I need more. I need to hear her say it one last time before it all goes to shit. "I need to hear you say it, Bec, please."

Her eyes find mine and I feel like she can see right into my soul. She brings her hand up to my cheek, resting it against me. I lean into her warmth. God, I will miss this.

"I love you Keegan Keller." Now comes the time where I will never hear her say those words again. I feel the tears I'm trying so desperately to hold back trying to break through but I just keep focusing on her hand and the comfort it is giving me.

"Something happened between me and Sarah," I say. Her hand doesn't move.

"Keegan, I kinda figured something happened when you moved out. At least you know what she's like and the type of person she is." My heart is telling me to just shut up and let it go. Leave it at this but my heart also knows she doesn't deserve more deception.

So I continue. "The night you hooked up with Tracey…" I feel her wince at my mention of him. "Well, when I left that night, I got hammered. Sarah called and I slept with her." And just like that, her hand is gone but not for long. Bec just slapped me hard across the face. I welcome the pain because it's better than what my heart is feeling right now.

"I love you, Bec…"

I hear her scuff at my words. She turns from me and is shifting through her draws behind her. She turns around and walks towards me. She puts something in my hand and I look down. My heart sinks. It's the locket I gave to her, not that I remember giving it to her. But this was my grandmother's and I know that there are pictures inside of it from when I first saw it on her. I didn't even notice she stopped wearing it.

"Bec, no. I don't want this back; I wanted you to have it. That's still what I

The Broken Girl

want. I know I screwed up but I love you." I beg her to keep it.

"You love me…"

I can hear the venomous tone and it makes me step back.

"Is that what you were telling yourself when you knowingly were screwing the brains out of the girl who drugged me. If that's love then I for damn sure don't want it. Fuck you, Keegan Keller! Fuck you."

I go to reach for her but she pulls back. Seeing the tears that now stain her cheeks is all it takes for the ones I had been holding back to break free.

"Please," I say.

> "How could you be with Sarah? You knew what she did to me!" She screams at me. "Please, tell me I can fix this," I plead.
>
> She is shaking her head and my heart is racing.
>
> "No, you can't. We are done, Keegan. Do you hear me? Done! I'm done with you.

The tears you see are not because I'm not over you. It's because you proved me right."

"God, Bec, I'm so sorry. Just please…" I'm barely able to keep myself from running to her and begging at her feet.

"What happened to us here, Keegan, is your fault! You kept pushing me away. I'm sorry it finally worked. I'm with Jake and now you are going to be alone. You can't hate me now that I'm moving on when you kept showing me you clearly had. Come to find out it was with the person who drugged me. You've lost me, Keegan."

I pull her to me, hoping the closeness will bring down her pain but it only makes it worse. However, I don't let go. I can't because I know this is all I am ever going to get. God, I love this girl.

"Get out, get out, get out! I hate you, Keegan. I hope you are happy now." God, happy is the last thing I am. "Get out!" She's screaming and is bawling.

Jake comes in and I turn my anger on him. "This is all your fault. If you'd just kept your mouth shut! Stay away from me, Jake. You finally did it. You stole the woman I love."

Jake doesn't respond the way I was hoping. "Key, go cool down. Give Becca space."

I let go of her and she just cuts me to the core. "I don't want space. I hate him. I never want to see him again." I can't handle it any more. I leave, closing the door behind me.

The Broken Girl

My feet can't seem to move. I'm frozen outside of her door. My hand is still holding the necklace I'd given her. It feels like an enemy, a reminder of everything I've lost. Everything I've let Sarah and myself take away from me. The only person who ever had my heart is screaming and crying not five feet from me. I can still hear everything.

"Jake, I'm so sorry I put you in the middle like that. Keegan is your friend but I just can't deal with him. I'm sorry. Charlotte has offered to go with me to my art courses and I think I need to get away. It doesn't mean I don't love you, because god knows I do. I love Keegan too, but I'm just too broken to deal with all of this, let alone spend a whole summer with those two so close to me. Don't hate me? Please." I can hear Bec sniffling through every word. I've wrecked her. The sobs that have erupted from my chest are my reminder of what I've done.

"Becca, I could never hate you. Maybe I will come and do a summer with you too. Get away from here. Just like before. Don't worry about me and Keegan," Jake says.

"I won't be the reason you two lose your friendship, Jake," Bec replies. This is one of the many reason I love this girl.

Gracie Wilson

"No, Becca, listen to me. I will always choose you." Why couldn't I just do that for her? Why did I have to be spiteful and go to Sarah? Knowing that if Bec ever found out it would be over. Maybe I haven't changed as much as I'd hoped. I still screwed up the best things that happen to me.

"Why couldn't he just remember me?" she cries.

"Becca, I can't fix this. I can't make him remember you." God, Jake, I wish you could, man. Because then I wouldn't have done all this stupid shit and screwed up my life.

"I see how much it hurts you Becca, which only hurts me more," Jake adds.

"Then we let him go." With Bec's words, I pull myself off the door and run out of the dorms into the cool night.

Chapter Twenty

Keegan

Everyone is just finishing the last exams, except for me. I was given an extension so that I could catch up on the material. I'm also going to take a course this summer. Originally it was refreshers, but now I see it as a way to keep busy. God, do I need that right now. Every day I see her, I want to run up to her, but I do as she asked. Bec doesn't look at me. She doesn't look at anyone. It's as if she's home, but the lights are all off. Her interest is nothing. I do know that Jake hasn't moved back into the dorms or staying with Bec at night. Drake told me, but only after I begged to know what was going on in her life. He told me about Jake instead, as a way to get around the 'Bec' issue.

To say that made me feel better would be an understatement. She told me I had pushed her to him and that's exactly what I expected. Now I don't really understand what's going on in her mind, but to know

Gracie Wilson

that she hasn't just went off to be with Jake is comforting. Not much, but enough to make me not want to shoot myself in the foot in order to feel pain anywhere, but in my heart. Being on my own in the apartment was great at first. But now it's just a constant reminder of the life I have lost. The distance all this shit has put between us is screwing with my head, the friends I still see only make that distance appear larger.

    I still haven't finished unpacking. Honestly, I've unpacked all the stuff that Alec and Drake packed, but the ones with Bec's handwriting on them remain untouched.

    Until today.

    I don't know why but I just felt like it was time. Opening the first box, I find some old t-shirts that I didn't really wear before except around the house. I pull one out and I instantly get the smell of Bec from it. Bringing it to my nose, the smell gives me comfort. These were on Bec, but then the fact that I have them again means she gave them back. There are pictures of the games, ones I don't remember, and a few other things that I'm not sure where they are from. Coasters from places I can't recall being at to add to my collection. I pick one up and it has a heart with 'Becca + Keegan' written

The Broken Girl

on it. Seeing my handwriting on this brings pain to my already screwed up heart.

    I open the second box, which is some of my CDs and posters. While taking them all out, I find a black tube, and I open it. It appears to be housing a poster, but the paper is too thick. Pulling it from its case, I unroll it. Looking back at me is myself. A sketch of me so detailed and personal that I don't have to look at the signature to know Bec did this, but there is more than one. The second one stops my heart and steals the breath in my lungs. Looking at this stirs memories that are begging to come back. There is a photograph of Bec and I in the forest. I am lying with my back on the ground and she is smiling down at me. She has taken this and painted it. It's perfect. I put it on my desk and make note to take it to get it framed tomorrow.

    I lift the box thinking it's empty and something slides in the box. It's one of my memories boxes from when I was younger. I open it, thinking I will be safe from memories of Bec. There are pictures of me in my hockey uniform as a child, and awards I'd won. At the bottom is an envelope that says 'Becca.' I lift the envelope, examining it. I know it's my handwriting but it's so strange because I don't know what's inside. Opening it, nothing prepared me for the royal mind fuck that is about to happen.

Dear Becca,

I wish I could say that you and I are fine. We both know that's not the case. Screwing us up is what I seem to do. None of it is your fault. I know I bring Michael up and throw him in your face. It's wrong, I know it, but it's what I do when I think I'm losing you.

When I saw you at the airport for the first time, you had me. I know you didn't know it then but my heart was already wrapped up in you. The day you called me, after Dillon had hurt you, I didn't know what was wrong but I knew you needed me. That gave me so much. I've never been needed, Becca. To be able to keep you safe was the only thing I've ever wanted since then.

I know that you know Sarah and I were together that summer. You always wondered why I went to her, and so did she. You think I didn't know about Jake, but I did. After three weeks without you, I got on a plane and came to find you. I missed you; being away from you was like my entire world was off course. But when I got there, I saw you and Jake walking into the hotel. You just

The Broken Girl

looked so happy. I loved you even then. As long as you were happy then I would suffer the heartbreak.

I wrote you a note and left something for you. At the last minute, I changed my mind. It would have been selfish to take that happiness from you to save my own heart. Never have I regretted that choice. Even now. If Jake wasn't good for you, I would have done everything to keep you apart. Seeing you become friends and then being inseparable was excruciating for me. I know you love me, but I think a part of you loves him too.

Does that mean I think we are over? Never. Not ever will that be our story, Becca. I've never believed in something as much as I believed in us. Although at the time when things got bad, I did hurtful things. I ran to Sarah, but I don't love her. Hell, I don't even like her most days. But there has always been something there with Sarah. I'm sorry that hurts you, but she isn't who I want or need. That's you.

Seeing you in the hospital after Dillon had attacked you (because of you running from me) was like someone ripped my heart out of my chest. I don't blame Jake for hating me or not letting me see you. Trust me; what my heart and head were doing to me was worse than anything he could do to me. When Alec snuck me in to see you and you just looked so broken and frail. I knew then I'd go to the end of the world for you; I'd take every pain you had and make it my own.

Saying her name. Well, it's inexcusable. There's nothing I can say to make you feel better about that. Only know that when I was with her… It was always you I saw. You're the only face I have ever seen when I look at a woman. You always say honesty is the only way with us so I'm being brutal. I do not blame you that you ran, after that. Between your heart being broken, I'm sure your heart is realizing you had feelings for Jake, and running was the best option. If I ever tried to stop you from running, it would mean I didn't really love the real you.

More than anyone, I understand the need for solitude. Don't ever think you need to explain it to me when you feel you need it. I've come a long way; I've made a lot of mistakes. To tell you that it will never happen again would only be setting us up for more pain. This I can promise you: no one will ever love you more than me. The person I was is gone. I've been becoming this person who lives to be a better man, and you're the reason for that.

The Broken Girl

This isn't enough; I'm not the person you deserve. But I promise to become that person. I think you'd be amazing for me and I know I'd be so good for you.

Anything I can do to make this up to you, Becca, just say the word and it's done. My problem was I went to the one who couldn't give me anything to save my heart. I forgot those who need me. Those people that I need more than the air I breathe. I've learned from my mistakes. I know I said I would change. Today's the day I can honestly say I've changed and you can believe it, Becca. I was such a fool to hurt you, because when I hurt you are the one I always turn to. I'm sorry I haven't been that person for you. I don't deserve you, Becca, but I'm asking you to let me have you anyway.

We've always had our ups and downs but, babe, we got this far. I'll do anything you want except be without you. This isn't the end for us; end isn't even a word known to our love. My life would never be the same without you. The only way I'd be able to survive one day without you in my life, is if I didn't know you. Don't give up on us, because I never will. I love you, Becca, so please just give us time.

Let's make every second count, babe.
Keegan

Inside, there is a dried Thistle and a note.

Becca,
I'm sorry I haven't been the person I was when we first met. I wanted you to stay that night in the airport, and not let you get on the plane. But begging you wouldn't have been fair. I never want to be the person to stop you. I wanted me to be that person, the one that made you want to stay. You have no idea how badly. But seeing you there I knew you need this. I'll see you in the fall, Becca.
Keegan.

My mind is reeling from everything in the note. I never knew the extent of what I had done to her, but seeing it now in the letter brings it all home for me. My heart still feels all those things, whether my mind does or not. My phone beeps and I know I have a text. Grabbing it, I see that it's from Charlotte.

Becca is leaving in the morning.

My heart jumps into my throat and I feel the panic set in. No, she can't leave. I need her to see this. She deserves to see this;

The Broken Girl

even if she hates me, she should know what she meant to me then as well as now. Running out of my bedroom with the notes in hand, I grab my keys off the counter and open the door. Sarah is standing there just about to knock. She smiles at me and my blood turns cold. I don't have time for this.

Moving around her, acting as if she isn't there, I shut the door and start walking away, leaving her eyes wide at my display.

"Key," she says.

"Sarah, I don't have time for your shit, I have to see Bec," I say without thinking.

She is stomping behind me. "What is it about her? She's just some whiny bitch. What's she got that I don't have? Why do you all run for her?" she yells.

I turn and walk right up to her. "She has a goddamn heart, that's what she has. This is all some game to you. You are screwing with people lives, Sarah. Does that not bother you? Bec has everything I will ever need, and you would never have something I'd want more than her," I yell back. She gets this sick twisted smile on her face, causing me to believe I just said the wrong thing.

"I'm pregnant." She says this in a tone that I'm not sure would qualify as happiness. She thinks she's won by this statement.

Turning around, I walk back to my apartment, shut the door in her face, and lock the door. Pacing in the kitchen, I think of just walking out and going to Bec anyway but she deserves so much more than this. I won't weigh her down with more shit that is entirely my fault. Grabbing my phone, I call the only person I can think of.

"Man, Sarah's pregnant. I know it's screwed up. I'm not saying I didn't sleep with her but I have to ask. Could it be yours?"

Chapter Twenty-One

Becca

After everything with Keegan, I just needed some 'me' time. Jake understood, but I never thought he'd do something so drastic. The plan was for him to come with me to Europe for my art program but then out of the blue, he changed his mind. Jake decided that he thought it would be better if I did this alone. I just need to get away and be 'Becca.' He wants me to get my head on straight before I jump into anything. Telling him I was sorry that I couldn't stay and that I was running away yet again was one of the hardest things I've ever said to Jake. I hate that I run but it's always been fight or flight for me. Fighting wasn't something I was ready to do just yet. He just told me to go and have an amazing time and he would see me too. So, I sat in the airport and said goodbye to Jake and Alec for six weeks. Charlotte and Drake came with me, of course. She wanted to see her family and Drake wanted to be with Charlotte.

I'd love to say that I talked to Jake often, but the longer I was gone, the more distance came between us. When my program finished I called Alec and told him I wasn't coming home for another three and a half months. Somewhere in the six-week course, I decided that I wanted to see if Scotland was my new home. I looked in to schools there for me to attend quietly, without Charlotte or Drake. I didn't want them to know or slip up around Alec. Charlotte and Drake headed back early to get settled in. They are moving in with Alec, and when I say moving in, I mean into a one bedroom. Together. I'm beyond thrilled for them. They are perfect for each other. To think back on the Drake I met and who he is now is mind-boggling.

When I stepped off the plane, I was shocked to find that no one was there waiting for me. I hadn't asked anyone, but I kind of expected it. I told Charlotte I was going to stop by their place before going to the dorms and get the rest of my things, but I still thought Jake or Alec would be here. Grabbing my bags, I exit the airport and get into a cab, giving him the address. When I pull up, nothing looks like it's changed. I know I have. This summer was eye opening

The Broken Girl

to me as to who I really am. Before I left, I decided on a school and even looked at attending as early as this winter semester.

Some of my paintings are even hanging up in a gallery. I was offered a full-time position and I seriously thought about taking my professor's offer. Painting does something to me. It's freeing. I've never felt more like myself than when a brush is in my hand. Also, I started photography and love playing with the images later. Distorting them and creating something new is a new type of art I've began working with these past few months.

Putting my key in the door, I can hear people inside but I think nothing of it. When I walk in and see everyone there, for a brief second I think it's a surprise party until they all turn around looking pale and shocked that I just walked in the door.

"Hey, guys," I say, happily.

Alec comes up and hugs me tightly. "Sorry, Becca. I must of lost track of time. Let me take you right over to the dorm and get you settled in."

Looking over my brother's shoulder, I see Jake and Keegan watching me. "Alec, what's going on here?" He doesn't say anything.

"Becca, let's get your stuff in Alec's car. You must be exhausted," Charlotte says. Drake is standing next to her and I can't get a read on him either.

"What is going on here, and why are you trying to rush me out of here? I get that I'm not Keegan's biggest fan, but that was five months ago. I can be an adult about this. We are all going to have to be around each other now with school and hockey season," I say to everyone.

"Well, I'm so glad to hear you say that, Becca." The voice makes my hair on the back of my neck stand up. I look to Drake first and he is just looking at me with such pity. Sarah just walked in and I wish that were the only shock. Her hand is on her belly.

"She's pregnant," I say.

Sarah laughs and just shakes her head. "Well, aren't you so smart." Her voice makes me want to hit her and I take a step forward, but Charlotte gets in my way.

"Becca," she warns.

"So, I hope this answers why they were trying to rush you out of here. They've been arguing for days about how to tell you this," Sarah snickers.

A light turns on in my head and I realize the only way her being knocked up would affect me is if it were Keegan's. My heart plummets. I'd love to say my summer away made the love I had for him disappear, but it didn't. This is the final nail in the coffin for him though.

"Okay, so when I said what's going on you were trying to figure out how to tell me Keegan knocked up Sarah. Well, it's none of my business what goes on between them, since he's moved on and so have I."

Both Keegan and Jake look to me at the same time. "You've done what?" They question me in unison.

Charlotte saves their feelings. "Relax, unless she met someone in the last ten days, she didn't mean there was actually someone else." I wouldn't have been so nice as to spare Jake and Keegan's feelings. Keegan screwed up all on his own. Jake, although we barely talked in the last month, even before that, it was just small talk.

"Well, there was her professor," Drake adds. Charlotte elbows Drake and I glare at him.

"Your professor?" Alec says.

"Drake is being a little over dramatic. My professor did ask me out once after classes had finished." I emphasize *once* so that my brother starts breathing again before I continue. "I said that it wasn't the right time for me to be getting involved, but that doesn't mean I won't. It just meant I wasn't ready. I worked at one of the galleries his work is in."

Drake starts laughing at the quietness around me. "Really if that kills the mood, let's drop the other bomb right now, Becca. Tell them about the painting."

I cringe because I know this is going to be an issue. "Well, not that it's anyone's business but he painted a portrait of me and it became quiet an important piece to his collection. It's being showcased in a collection that's touring right now." Jake and Keegan are watching me closely. Alec just looks confused until he seems to move on from this.

Jake looks at me oddly. "What were you doing in the portrait, Becca?" Drake starting chuckling hysterically again and I make a mental note to kick him later.

"None of your business." What I did in Europe is no one's business.

Sarah is giggling and I look to see her on her phone. "Well, Becca, aren't you the little hottie." Everyone looks to Sarah. "What I just googled her program and they have it on here what her professor is showcasing. Then once I clicked it, I could see his work." Keegan grabs her phone from her. When he looks, his face goes red. Jake and Alec follow suit, looking at her phone.

The Broken Girl

"Before you three have an aneurism, you can't tell it's me and nothing is shown," I say, hoping to make everyone relax.

"You are naked," Alec says.

"No, my back is to the picture so you can't see my breast or my bottom, which is covered by the sheet." Keegan is silent and it's a good thing because he has nothing he can say.

"You got naked for your professor who asked you out, but you wouldn't go on a date with him. Think you have that backwards, Becca. He should buy you dinner before you get naked for him," Jake sneers.

"Jake, really. I thought that out of everyone, you would understand the beauty of her portrait. It's beautiful and I am so proud of her. You have no idea what it took for her to do this, and the fears she had to overcome," Charlotte defends.

"No, Charlotte, it's fine. He's allowed to be angry. But maybe if he had talked to me about what was actually going on in my life, instead of small talk, he'd have known," I shoot back.

"Alec," I say softly. My brother needs to understand this.

"It's beautiful, Becca. I know you would never do something if it was of ill taste," he says. I hug him. Alec will always be one of my biggest supporters, but he's tied with Charlotte, of course.

"Keegan, I know this will be awkward but if you and Sarah are happy, then that's all that matters." Keegan goes pale and quickly looks at Jake before looking back at me, but I still notice.

"So no one is going to tell her," Sarah says. I back away from them all; they all know something and are hiding it from me.

"Bec, I'm not with Sarah."

My heart sinks when I look at Jake.

"Becca, we didn't know how to tell you. We wanted to figure everything out first." No, not Jake.

"You are with Sarah. What the hell! I went to Europe and came back to an alternate reality."

I saw his confusion. "No, I'm not with Sarah."

"Okay, now I'm just confused." My heart has recovered to the shock it felt when it thought Jake and Sarah were together.

"Bec, I could be the father," Keegan states. I'm not shocked because I knew they had slept together.

"Becca, I may be the father." My brother then says.

"What?" My brother has moved in front of me. I turn away from them right into

The Broken Girl

Jake's arms and he hugs me. If Alec is the father, I will never be rid of Sarah.

"Oh, come on now... let's not forget the best part, Jake," Sarah laughs.

My head looks right up into his eyes, begging them to tell me something.

"Becca, I love you." My heart seems to be dealing because those words make me hopeful.

"I could be the father too, Becca." Just like that, my heart is shattered on the floor by Jake's words.

Chapter Twenty-Two

Keegan

Seeing her fall to pieces in front of my eyes was like a glass shard being jammed into my gut.

"No," was all Bec said.

Charlotte and Drake stand by, not knowing what to do or say. At this moment, I don't think there really are any words that would give comfort.

"Becca," Jake begs. She backs away from him and I'm surprised to find her at my side. She looks shyly at me and I wish I could read her mind. Looking into those beautiful crystal eyes, I see the pain we have all caused her.

"Let me explain," Jake says.

"No, Jake, just shut up."

Her words cut him deep and he steps back. "Becca, I honestly don't know what we are supposed to say here." Alec tries to reach her with his words. She just looks around, lost. What have we done to her?

The Broken Girl

"Well, looks like you all have some issues to work out now, don't you. Becca, I'd love to say sorry but... well, I'm not." Sarah's words are full of sarcasm.

She did this on purpose. I can't prove it but I know she wanted to hurt Bec. I just never thought she'd do something like this. But I shouldn't be that surprised by the depth this girl will go.

"Listen and listen good, Sarah. You may be off limits now." She takes a step towards her and Jake steps in, protecting Sarah. The hurt in Bec's eyes at Jake's protectiveness makes me get choked up at the life we've just handed her.

"I see," Bec says, but it doesn't stop her. "Well, one day, Sarah. One day very soon, the baby won't protect you. One day you will see that you are nothing more than a skank who has not only ruined her own life, but that of her child. You think you've won, but all you've done is put a big target on your back. You had better pray this child is Keegan or Jake's. If it's Alec's, you will have a lifetime with me and I will make every single day of it miserable for you." The look on Sarah's face tells me she knows this wasn't a threat but a promise. My heart broke when she said she'd only have to deal with Sarah if it was Alec's baby. That means that she's done with us.

Sarah starts crying and runs into the kitchen. "Attention seeking like always, Sarah." Bec says loudly enough for Sarah to still hear it.

"That's enough, Becca!" Jake yells at her.

Without thinking, I put an arm protectively around Bec. "No, Jake. I think you've said and done enough. We just dropped a bomb on her and you expect her to do what? Say congratulations?" He looks right at me and the hate I see in his eyes doesn't make me less angry with him.

"Don't be mad at me that you screwed this up too. Guess Jake's not as perfect as he pretends to be."

"Wrong move, Key." Jake goes to get in my face. I see Drake move away from my side to intercept Jake, but then something crazy happens.

Bec steps from beside me where she had been and is now between Jake and I. She isn't protecting Jake.

"That's not going to happen," she says, with such strength it makes me wonder who this strange creature is. Jake looks mystified at her reaction, with his fists still clenched and ready to hit me.

The Broken Girl

"Leave Keegan alone," Bec says, grabbing my hand while never moving from in front of me. He looks like she has just slapped him but her hand never left mine.

"This is how it's going to be." Jake turns and storms off into his room, slamming the door.

Charlotte steps forward but Bec shakes her head. "Let him go," Bec says.

Drake gets up, grabbing his keys. "I will take Sarah home. I'm thinking she's done enough damage." I nod at him but Bec just stares off.

"Charlotte, you should go with him. We know she has no idea of boundaries." Bec's words are laced with hate.

"I wouldn't be that mean to Drake and make him be alone with that thing." Charlotte smiles at Bec and leaves to the kitchen with Drake to get rid of Sarah, thankfully.

"Becca, are you okay?" Alec looks torn and I feel for him. I doubt he thought this would be what was going to happen.

"No I'm not okay, but I guess I shouldn't be surprised though. Guys always take the easy route. Well now you three have a huge problem." Quickly I squeeze her hand, hoping she won't let go. She looks to me and I see that she understands how much I need her to just be here with me right now.

"Alec, I don't get how you could do that with her after everything she's done to me."

Bec is talking in anger and I feel for her. At a time like this, I wouldn't be as calm as she is.

"Becca, it's not like she tried to off you or anything. She just tried to steal Keegan from you. She wanted to take love away from you. I wasn't her goal, but I was just convenient.

"Really, she didn't do anything to me? What do you call drugging me at a party to get me out of the way?!" She yells this at Alec before she realizes what she's done. She looks at me, panicking.

"What are you talking about?" He looks at me and I wish Sarah was here to deal with the wrath that's about to happen.

"Alec, can I just say that this is a really bad time to get into this, man, but Sarah gave Bec some party favours at a party to get her out of the way. It was around the time I slept with her, when we all slept with her. We didn't tell you because we didn't want you to tell your parents and Bec end up being back home alone. You know she didn't want that."

Alec is working through it all, and I know he wants to be mad that he didn't

The Broken Girl

know, but he's working on his big brothering. "Becca, I wish you had told me. I wish you thought you could tell me without me going off the deep end. She won't get away with this. Her days of having us three running for her is done. Well, at least I'm done. Until we know who's the father and until that baby is born, I'm not doing anything. She isn't welcome here, Key. I know you just moved back in but she can't be around Becca…"

I cut Alec off before he can give the same speech. "Man, trust me, I was done with her long ago. If the baby is mine, I will do whatever I can for my child, but I won't be around Sarah. She made this a game; I'm done playing it. Bec's feelings and her safety mean more to me than anything," I add, to show her that I'm serious. Nothing has changed for me.

Alec looks at me and smiles. We've talked about Bec while she was gone. He knows I still love her.

"Alec, I know that I hid it from you, and I'm really sorry. All I could think about was Becca having to leave. Funny thing is that's all I want now." Alec's smile drops and I assume I have the same look of horror on my face. Leave? She can't leave. She just got back.

"Alec, I'm going to talk to Keegan for a bit. Then I'll head over to the dorm."

He walks up and gives her a hug. "I'm so glad you're home, Becca." He walks out of the house, leaving us alone. My palms are sweating ever since she let go of my hand and said she was leaving.

"Bec. We really do need you here." She gives a sad smile that doesn't reach her eyes. I've learned this is when she is trying to fake it for other's benefit.

"You also know how much it is to ask me to stay. School starts tomorrow so we don't have to worry about me leaving until the end of the school year. So, since I know you will tell me the truth, what the hell happened?"

The fact that she just told me I have eight months to change her mind makes me want to give her the brutal truth.

"Well, you know that I slept with Sarah the night I saw you at the bar. Your brother slept with her the day before the party we all went to. Jake hasn't said anything about when it happened, but he said he's a possibility too. The night before you were going to leave, I was coming to see you, and I wanted to make it right. Do something to ensure that I hadn't lost you; you've become my light, Bec. If I didn't have your friendship I'd be lost."

The Broken Girl

She doesn't recoil from me, this makes me happy, but it's laced with sadness. What I really want to tell her is that I loved her before the accident and I love her now. This would only cause her further pain and push her away. I won't risk losing her forever. This, I can do, if it means I get to keep a piece of Bec.

Bec takes my hand and holds it tightly. Her ability to know what I've always needed from her is amazing. "I had heard about a rumour that Jake and Sarah had something happen. Don't kill me. I just found out earlier that day but I wasn't sure what to do. I thought it was Sarah causing shit. I never thought Jake would actually risk that."

She shakes her head and I see tears in her eyes. "Me either," she whispers.

"I called Jake right after she told me, asking him if it could be his."

Her eyes snap up to mine at what I just said. "What?" I ask.

"Jake knew before I left? You told him the night before I left? Are you sure?" Her eyes are begging me to say that he didn't know.

"Yes. He knew, Bec, but so did I. How could we tell you this, then have you leave? You'd have never come back." She nods in reply and my heart crashes. "We don't know if there could be more possibilities, Bec. We were trying to talk her into doing a paternity test now." Looking at her, I just want to hold her and never let her go. Small steps though. "Come with me, I want to show you something." I point to my room and she follows me.

As soon as we walk in, she spots what I wanted her to see. Looking back at us is the painting she did of us. "I know I didn't say anything when you told us about your portrait. Honestly, I'm surprised you're in one and not doing them. You're so talented, but you're beautiful too. Of course someone would want to capture that for the rest of the world. Right now I see that you're crying and you are still the most beautiful person I've ever seen." Her eyes still haven't left the painting hanging beside my bed. She slowly backs up and sits on my bed; I sit next to her and try to steady my breathing. I know if I leaned over and kissed her right now, she wouldn't stop me. But that would be selfish with everything going on right now. I want all of her, not just right now, but always.

"Bec, I'm not asking you to love me or to even try to love me again. But please just tell me I haven't lost you because it would kill me if that friendship was gone." My voice is shaky and I just want to touch her so

The Broken Girl

badly. She does the unthinkable. She turns to me and kisses me lightly on my lips. I feel the wetness from her tears. I don't do anything to deepen the kiss. I just let her have this.

"You haven't done anything unforgivable and you were honest with me. That's all I've ever asked. You don't treat me as breakable and you don't hide things from me. I know you didn't tell me because you didn't want me to stay away. You are right, I wouldn't have come back."

I nod and she brings her forehead to rest against mine. "Bec, you will never know how sorry I am for everything I've done to you."

"I do know, because you choose to tell me the truth no matter the consequences. You didn't act selfishly; you left it up to me. For that reason, Keegan, you haven't lost me."

Whatever happens, I won't ask for more from her. I will be the best friend she could ever have. The tears are coming fast down her cheeks and I feel my tears follow suit. Look what we've gotten into, but above all, look what I haven't lost. As long as I still have Bec, I can get through this.

Chapter Twenty-Three

Becca

    Sitting in the room with Keegan brought so many things back. The way it used to be between us and how easy it would be to just go back to that. So many other things I wish were dead and buried. I don't know why I kissed him but I just felt it was needed. He's hurting, I'm hurting, and it brought us comfort.
    "Bec, those words…your friendship means everything to me. I won't put it in jeopardy again. These last five months have been the worst of my life. Before you left, I was done with Sarah's games. You are more important to me than any of this. If you are happy without me in your life. As long as you are happy I'm happy. Although I'm really hoping you'd be happier with me around because my life hasn't been the same without you." Keegan's words are true. This Keegan is someone I've just recently begun to figure out. He protects me, puts me first.

The Broken Girl

Even when his own heart is left in shambles. He is someone I will protect.

"What are you going to do about Sarah?" I ask him.

He just shakes his head and brings his hands to his face. "Am I horrible if I say I don't want to talk about her or think about a future with her? Can I just lay here with you?" If my heart wasn't so broken, it would melt at the sweetness of Keegan. Truthfully, it does, but I'm not ready to admit it. I nod and shuffle back into the bed, lying down. He follows me and lies down beside me. He looks uncomfortable as if he doesn't know where to put his hands. Shifting, I bring my head and rest it over his heart. He wraps his arms around me. He needs comfort, but most of all he needs truth.

"You won't lose me, Keegan. I think you need me as much as I need you."

We stay this way, feeling the comfort of each other. I must have nodded off because when I look to the clock it's been three hours since I got here. Keegan is fast asleep. I contemplate staying here like this, but that would only lead to more confusion. Quietly and slowly, I slide out of his grasp. He moves, trying to find me again. In his sleeping state, he snuggles a pillow and I exit the room, closing the door and thinking of the cuteness of Keegan. I turn to see Jake sitting on the couch, looking right at me. Guilt overwhelms me but I push it aside. I've done nothing wrong but comfort a friend, who is so lost at the moment that he doesn't know which way is up.

Walking around the couch as if I don't see him, I hear him get up. "So, you will talk to him, but not me."

I stop and turn to see Jake watching me, gauging my emotions. "Jake, I'm tired. I have to get back to my place."

He just glares at me and I know I'm not leaving any time soon. "My bed used to be your place." I feel like I've been hit in the gut knocking the wind out of me.

"Well, that was before I realized it wasn't just me you were inviting in there." I lash out back at him.

"That's not fair. I told you I had slept with someone."

"I never thought it would be her, so why her, Jake? You had to know it would kill me knowing she'd been with you. What about all those times you told me she was horrible? Why say that about her and send her away only to do this. Please just tell me it's not true. Tell me this is some way of protecting me… just say it." My heart is racing.

The Broken Girl

"Becca, I wish I could, believe me. It's why I didn't tell you." His look begs me. I want to scream at him but it won't solve anything.

"Do you want it to be your baby?" He just stares at me, not answering me. I know the damage is done. "When did it happen, Jake?"

"Does it matter?" He looks torn but I push him harder.

"When? I deserve that, don't I? He nods and his words are like knives.

"The night of the party."

"When she drugged me?"

I am doing everything to keep myself calm. Jake just looks down and nods. "So I guess she just wasn't trying to get me out of the way for Keegan. Funny though, I never knew I was in the way with you, Jake. You were the one I knew more than anything I loved and you loved me too. That's gone now."

He jumps up and runs to me, placing his hands on my arms. "Don't say that, Becca."

"Jake, what did you expect? Was this before or after you walked away from me while I was calling out for you?" Please say before.

"Right after." Just like that, it's over.

"Jake, I would have followed you anywhere. Done anything for you. Right now I don't know what you want me to say other than I can't accept this. I won't. If you ask me, I don't think you love me like you say you do," I respond.

"Becca, I do love you and I will always love you. But she could be carrying my child. You can't hate me for wanting to be there for her. If I wasn't, I wouldn't be the person you love." Turning away from him, I try and catch my breath.

"Loved," I whisper.

"You can't stop loving someone just like that, Becca," Jake says defensively.

"Yes, I can, and you know why? I was lying there unconscious, in possible danger, and you were screwing the girl that put me in that position. Keegan told me he called you to come and you didn't until you knew how bad it was. Why, Jake? Was he interrupting?"

Jake takes a step away from me looking hurt. "It didn't mean anything, but I cannot walk away from my obligations now." Hating him for this would be easy, but I understand a part of this.

"You know what she's done to me, but you stand by her?" He just nods.

"When Keegan called you the night before I left, you were still planning on

The Broken Girl

coming. Was his call the reason you told me to go alone? Did you lie to me, and make it out to be like I needed it?" Jake's fist clench and I know I've struck a nerve.

"Yes. I wanted to figure it out, but then you didn't come home and I figured it would be better to find out in person."

"No, Jake. It would be better if this wasn't even an option. Of everyone in my life, I've always depended on you. Well, that's it. You've done something we can't fix. I'm done." I start walking away but he grabs my arm, turning me around to him.

"I missed the hell out of you, Becca." I feel for him because I know he's trying to remind me of our history. Unfortunately, Sarah might be his future and this angers me.

"Was that before or after you screwed the one person I hate. God, Jake, if it were anyone else I would be able to deal. You're such a fuckhead! I don't know why I'm surprised. Whenever something good happens, it all goes to hell. I just didn't think you'd be the one doing the irreparable damage, Jacob."

"We had something beautiful and you turned it to shit. Twice now, this despicable woman has ruined me. Taken those I love from me. Now you stand by her, and now you want to be the father of her child. I would understand dealing with her once you know it's your child, like my brother and Keegan plan on doing. That's the problem though. They know that if they're the dad, they are stuck with her. They don't want that. I just never thought it would be you I'd lose to her. That night meant everything to me. I gave you everything I had, but that's all I could give you. It wasn't enough. We're over, Jake. " My voice is giving away how much this is hurting me.

"No, what we did and what I felt…that doesn't just end. I won't let you end us, Becca." Jake takes a step forward and I move, putting distance between us.

"Jake, when I was gone, all I wanted was less distance between us. I thought it was because I was gone. Come to find out I've never felt more distant to you than I do right now standing five feet away from you," I say.

"No, you're not ending us." He continues to argue.

"You did this. You're nothing more than a liar, Jake. You say you hid this from me so you didn't lose me. Well, Keegan didn't and that's why he hasn't lost me. But it looks like you have. I'm giving up on you, Jake, because clearly you've given up on me." With that, I walk out the door holding my head high. He may not think I have a

The Broken Girl

right to be upset, but I know I deserve better and it's time I start acting like it.

Walking away from the house, I hear the door open and close behind me. Mentally I start preparing for another round with Jake.

"Let me take you home, Becca?" I turn to see Drake and Alec standing there.

"You heard everything, didn't you?" They both nod. "Well, then you know I'm emotionally exhausted and I just want to go home." My brother opens the door for me and Drake gets in the back with me.

"Becca, for what it's worth, they both still love you." I smile to Drake at his kind words however minimal they are.

"That's what makes it so much more painful." As we pull away, the tears start to fall. I'd done so well hiding them from Jake.

When we get there, Drake and Alec hug me. Drake looks at me and I know he's going to say something he thinks I might hate him for. "I think you need to realize Jake might not be this person you made him out to be. No one can live under that type of pressure. He loves you, Becca. He was only trying to spare your feelings."

I look at him, hoping my words don't fail me. "I think you are right, Drake, but I've determined that no matter the best intentions, lying to those you love is never the answer. I'll find someone, someone that loves me enough to not make me cry."

He gives me a tight squeeze. "Maybe hottie professor." He chuckles and I laugh at his words too. He leaves me and gets back in the car.

"Becca, I'm sorry for tonight. There is so much to deal with and it's mostly my fault." Alec is the last person who should be apologizing.

"Alec, you all thought with your dicks instead of your brains. I'd love to say that this will all be okay, but it won't." All I want is to move on from this.

"I will do anything I can to help you and Keegan, but that's all I can do. I won't be around her. She's done something I will never forgive or forget." Looking up into the night sky, I'm wishing I were anywhere but here. For a second I think I've said it out loud because of Alec.

"Becca, you can't stay here out of guilt." With those words, I know my brother just set me free. He gave me everything at that moment.

He told me he wouldn't stop me from leaving.

Chapter Twenty-Four

Becca

Charlotte and Drake have been hovering over me for the last several weeks. Getting back into classes and group projects was overwhelming with all the added drama. I haven't spoken to Jake the entire time. He's stayed away and I haven't gone looking. Keegan and I are making a try at being friends. He handles it well, considering the guys who have come around. Although that may be because I continue to shoot them all down. My heart just isn't in it. Classes are boring and I miss art daily. I've found that my books are full of sketches and new supply lists for painting more than actual notes.

To say I haven't thought about leaving Thunder Bay every single day since my brother told me not to stay out of guilt, would be lying. I'm waiting for something; I just don't know what exactly that is yet. Somehow I feel that there will be this fleeting moment where everything comes together and I know I'm making the right choice. Bad choices are something I just can't afford any more. Keeping busy has been my main goal. I find myself less stir crazy then. When I say I'm studying in my room, I'm really painting and working on new techniques. Getting lost in each stroke and not having to use my words to explain everything is a new type of freedom.

 Keegan and Alec stopped taking my excuses a few days ago when they realized I'd walked into my class with paint on me. Did I mention Keegan is the teacher's assistant in one of my classes? Busted… So now here I am. Today is the first game I've been able to make it to. Sitting in the crowd, I feel disconnected. Last year I was, whether I knew it or not, in love with two of the players. Now I'm just a regular spectator or at least that's what I tell myself. Watching the men warming up, who have broken my heart more times than I can count, is frustrating. On one hand, I'm happy to just be seeing Jake. On the other hand, I never want to look at him again. Keegan is just different lately, in an amazing sort of way.

 Sarah is sitting a few benches over and lower than me. Her belly is growing every day. She still hasn't agreed to the testing yet. She keeps coming up with reasons to put it

The Broken Girl

off. 'I'm tired. I don't feel well. Maybe next week.' I know what she's doing. Thinking she can have the three of them jumping when she calls. My brother doesn't even answer any more. He told her when he sees the results, he will help, and only with the child. After everything that came to light, he told her in more ways than one exactly how it was going to go with him being the father. He even threatened to use my drugging as a way to get full custody.

Keegan, she came around a bit at first, but he made it clear that he will never have anything to do with her. Not now, not ever, and no matter the results. He didn't need to be in her life to be a father. We talked about it because I wanted to make sure he wasn't doing this for me. If he wanted to be a part of this, I wouldn't stop him. Watching the boys continue to warm up, I notice Keegan waving me down to one of the doors that are still open to the rink.

Getting down, I go to him. He looks so much like the guy I met almost two years ago but somehow I feel more connected now than I did when we were together. "Bec, I was hoping you'd show up." I sigh because I know this is my fault. Every time there was a game, I would come up with something. Seeing this just brought back so many memories good and bad. Taking off his helmet, he shakes out his hair and my senses are overwhelmed. Keegan let his hair grow out a bit longer than he usually chooses to keep it. I can't say I don't like it either.

"You've got helmet hair, Keegan."

Keegan laughs at me and shakes my hair with his glove. Smiling up at him, I see we've come further than I thought. "Now we both have messy hair, but you still look amazing. I'm just a smelly hockey player." Without thinking, I lean in, smelling him.

I smile at him. "No, you smell like Keegan."

He chuckles at me. "Does this mean Keegan smells like a smelly hockey player?" He smirks.

I smack him for his flirting but answer him anyway. "No, it means you smell amazing and I'd jump you here if it wasn't a crowded arena." Giving him my best sassy smile, I pull his jersey so he comes towards me, giving him a tight hug.

"You don't play fair, Bec." He laughs against me.

"You got this, Keegan, go show them who is boss." I wink at him.

Keegan surprises me by quickly kissing me on the lips and starts skating away. "Who's boss now, Bec?" I laugh but stop when Keegan ends up face first in the ice.

The Broken Girl

"KEEGAN!" I yell.

"Key, get your head on straight, it's game time." Jake just came up from behind Keegan, checking him.

Alec helps Keegan up and is now yelling at Jake. "Get to the bench, Jake! What the hell man? Get your shit together." Jake just looks at me and skates off to the bench. Alec was named Captain this year. Alec looks at me and I wave Keegan over.

"Keegan, I'm so sorry. I don't get what the hell is going on with him. I haven't even talked to him in weeks." I bring my fingers and graze them over the reddening mark on his cheek.

"Bec, his problem is that you haven't talk to him but you are talking to me. Touching me." Quickly, I pull my hand away from him.

"So, it's my fault. God, I'm so stupid," I say, shaking my head. Keegan takes his glove off and stills me by placing his hand against the side of my face.

"No, you're not stupid, Bec. Confused, maybe. Never stupid. Don't worry about Jake and me. This isn't our first argument. As long as it's for something worth it, I don't mind." Leaning in to Keegan's warm hand, I remind myself of all the drama that lies ahead of us.

"I'm not, Keegan. With everything in your life I'm the last thing that would be worth it, trust me." Giggling brings us back to reality and I see Sarah. "She's not worth it, but you definitely are." Keegan skates off this time to avoid being hit by his own team.

Once I'm back in my seat, Charlotte has joined me. "You have this goofy grin on your face, Rebecca Potts." She winks at me.

"I do not." Trying to take the smile off my face proves to be difficult, so I give up and we breaking out in laughter.

"Becca, one day soon you and that heart of yours are going to have to figure all this out."

Nodding in reply, I look around as the boys take the ice. "Today is not that day, Charlotte."

She puts her arm around me, holding me close. "No, it's not."

The team plays a close game for the first two periods, but you can tell there is something going on between Keegan and Jake. By the third period, we are ahead. There are five minutes left on the board and Keegan makes an amazing save. I jump up screaming and he looks right at me. Laughing and jumping with Charlotte, we both blow him kisses and he catches them with his glove. Jake comes up beside him, tripping him with his stick. Keegan goes

The Broken Girl

down flat on his back; he quickly gets up and pushes Jake. The gloves come off and their teammates are struggling to get them off each other. Helmets are gone. Keegan has a busted lip and Jake will definitely have a black eye later.

The referee is blowing his whistle and yelling. "Twenty-two and twelve, you're both out of the game." The referee yells, pointing to the dressing room doors.

"They're on the same damn team!" the coach yells.

The guys get off the rink, still yelling at each other. Alec looks at me and gives me a dirty look telling me I'm in big shit later.

"Well, that can't be good," Charlotte says, with a smirk on her face, and I playfully smack her. The team does some position switches and continues. They almost lose with the other goalie in. He's no Keegan, that's for sure. But they make it by the skin of their teeth. Everyone cheers but they are still talking about the craziness of the fight.

We make our way to the area where we wait for the guys to come out and I see them both exit. They are still arguing. Alec walks up behind them, smacking them both on the back of their heads.

Sarah rushes over. "Jake, are you okay?" She says actually sounding like she cares. If I didn't know her, I'd think she did. I turn to head out and wait for everyone, away from this woman, and I stop dead in my tracks.

"Rebecca." Standing in front of me is the last person I'd ever expect to be there.

"Professor Hunt."

Chapter Twenty-Five

Standing there, I'm shocked at the sight before me.

"Rebecca, I haven't been your teacher for a very long time. What happened to you calling me Trevor?"

Giving him a shy smile, I look around at everyone watching us. "Trevor, sorry you just surprised me." Standing before me, he's tall and dressed in a pair of grey dress pants and a white button up shirt, with the top buttons undone. He has the most penetrating grey eyes. With his blonde hair, saying he's attractive would be an understatement.

"Sorry, Rebecca, I didn't mean to sneak up on you," he says. And the sound of his voice is enough to give every girl shivers.

"Becca." Alec is staring at me and I realize I haven't introduced him formally.

"Everyone, this is Trevor Hunt. He's the artist that did my portrait in Paris this summer." Jake and Keegan are watching Trevor very closely.

"Your professor," Jake states.

"That's actually why I'm here. The painting is being showcased in Toronto and, well, I want you to join me." Just like that, six jaws drop, but not mine.

"Really, you want me to go to the showcase?"

He laughs, sweetly nodding.

"I'd love to go, Trevor. I've been to so many in Europe and I'd love to see the workings of one locally."

"I was hoping you'd say that, Rebecca. I was hoping we could also disclose that you are in fact the model." This makes me tense. I hadn't really thought about that part of it. People might notice the resemblance.

"I don't know, Trevor. You know how I am in a crowd, and I don't like the attention being on me." I shift nervously.

"How many times do I have to tell you that beauty can't be hidden, amazement can't be dulled, and love can't be demolished?" His words are something I'd grown to enjoy while I was away. Hearing them now, in front of everyone, was something I wasn't ready to deal with.

"If you don't want people to know, Rebecca, I would never tell anyone of course. But you are doing the world an incredible injustice by taking yourself away from them. You should be shown, displayed, celebrated."

The Broken Girl

"Sorry to interrupt but aren't you not allowed to date students?" Jake says rudely.

"Actually, it's a program, not a university. It's not exactly something they'd like to see but it isn't disapproved of. Besides all that, I'm no longer a professor there and Rebecca will never again be a student. She's incredible gifted and has an amazing future ahead of her. One she won't be able to fulfill here." You've got to give it to Trevor. He can handle whatever is thrown at him with ease.

"I think we are well aware of what her future entails. We've known her for much longer," Jake snipes back.

"You look very young to be a professor?" Alec says.

"Trevor is only twenty-six." I say. "He graduated early with a double major of Marketing and Art, followed by a Masters, of course."

Jake chuckles. "Starving artist, eh?"

I glare at Jake. "Jacob, really?"

Trevor just grabs my hand softly then let's go. "Hardly. Rebecca doesn't like to brag, however, I will have no issues with that. Along with being thoroughly educated, I also own my own marketing firm that just went global. So, starving? Never. I also wouldn't be asking Rebecca to come work for me if I didn't think it would be profitable for her, along with working at the Gallery, of course." Jake is speechless at Trevor's words.

"Jake, if Trevor decided to retire today, his family wouldn't have to worry about money for generations," I add, usually I wouldn't play this sort of game but the looks I'm getting are frustrating me to no end.

"Rebecca, I just got in but I was hoping to see some of the work you've been doing. Can I go check in at the hotel and then meet you at your place, unless you would like to come to my place?" he asks.

The group is watching hanging on every word, looking for me to flinch or run. "Actually, that would be perfect, so why don't you check in and I will text you my address. I live in the dorms, and I hope that won't be an issue. It will be easier than dealing with bringing my paintings to you."

Trevor smiles at me and waves his phone at me. "Not a problem, I'll go get checked in and wait for your message. Nice to see you again, Charlotte and Drake." With that, Trevor leaves me unknowingly to deal with this. Is it too late to run off with him? Turning around, I see everyone watching me closely.

"Okay, so before I discuss anything, I don't believe it's any of your business but it

The Broken Girl

definitely isn't Sarah's. So if you want to ask me anything, the incubator has to leave."

She glares at me but then just laughs it off. "You two idiots were fighting over her in a hockey game and in comes Mister rich Professor. Guess it's not just the two of you competing for 'Rebecca' any more. Becca, take my advice. I can't steal him from you, so he's the safe bet." With that, she hobbles off, leaving me to deal with her words.

"Okay what do you want to know?"

"So, you're letting a stranger come to your dorm room and what? Hang out?" Jake snaps.

"Actually, he isn't so different from you, Jacob. We spent the summer together so since you had no issue with you being in there, I think your point is moot."

Keegan chuckles. "She's got a point there, and I don't even remember that shit and it made sense to me." Everyone other than Jake laughs.

"If this is the road you want to go down, let's hope you know what you are doing, Rebecca." He drags out my name to mimic Trevor.

"What I'm doing? Don't act like you care about what I'm doing. You're just scared to see that maybe I'm better off without you. The job offer, the life away from here, it's tempting and I just might take it to get away from this freak show." I snap at Jake.

"Damn, I don't even know who you are any more, Becca?"

"I don't think you ever knew who I was, because you wouldn't have hurt me like you did. I can say this for certain; I don't think I ever really knew you, Jacob Kelso, because that person would have been happy that someone was expressing interest in my work, and my intelligence. You tell me how gifted I am yet you don't understand how others could think the same."

He laughs in a hateful tone. "Don't kid yourself. The only thing he's interested in is what's between your legs, and maybe you've already given him what he wants." He turns and starts to walk.

"What the hell is wrong with you, Jake?" Alec yells, causing him to stop. I put my hand on Alec, stopping him. "No, Jake, the one who gets down and dirty with anyone is clearly not me. I'm not the one who's storming off because he can't deal with the drama he caused by putting his parts in a woman he didn't love."

Turning away, I walk back into the arena area and sit down on the seat in front of the empty rink, which is now being cleaned by the Zamboni. I put my head in

The Broken Girl

my hands, trying to calm my rage. Jake just has this way of getting under my skin and staying there. He's never been this hateful or hurtful towards me. It's giving me a whole new side to Jake. An arm goes over me and I look up expecting Jake. Don't ask me why, but hope was all I had.

"Bec, are you okay? That got pretty nasty back there." Keegan just looks at me and his eyes are so bright that I forget for a minute why my heart feels trampled.

"Oh, that. Jake's never going to be okay with anything I do. I'm never going to be okay with him and Sarah. So that doesn't really leave much to talk about, does it?" Keegan looks uncomfortable and I realize he can take what I said about Jake to mean the same for him.

"No, Keegan, you never lied to me. You didn't protect her over me. You don't ask me to be pleasant or to have to deal with her like he expects me to. You understand my hurt, you feel my pain." I try to convey how much it all means to me.

"Of course, I do. When will you understand that your pain is my pain too, Bec," he replies and I rest my head on his shoulder. "Everyone is going to try and talk you out of going to the showcase, Bec, but I think you need to do this. Show him your work, step into the light, be the girl I know and love. You can't hide forever. I won't let you. The world deserves to know you," Keegan adds.

"But with everything going on, it just is bad timing," I respond.

"This mess will still be here when you get back, and so will everything with Jake. You need to see it through. Don't leave it unfinished. Whoever you may end up with, Bec, as long as they know how good they have it, and you are happy, then it will have all been worth it." I turn, seeing the pain it is giving him to say this. Why did I ever believe we could only be friends? If that's what he wants and needs, I will do anything. Keegan has lost everything, so I will give him this. If that means dealing with Jake, I will do that too.

"Please tell me that one day my life won't be filled with all this uncertainty and chaos." He lets out a long sigh and I know he's thinking about this day too.

"Trevor isn't bad. If anything, he gets you, which is exactly what you need right now. He's right though, Bec. You deserve everything and if you are not happy here…well, I'd never ask you to stay. Never sacrifice your happiness, for my gain."

My heart is racing at his words because, for a minute, I feel like he's saying goodbye and that he doesn't need me like I need him. "Wherever you go, Bec, that doesn't change us. It never will."

***

Standing in my dorm room, waiting for Trevor to show up, is unnerving. I've never had another man in here. Keegan was amazing as per his usual. Seeing him handle Trevor the way he did was a new experience. Prior to the accident, he would have acted like Jake. The irony that they have switched places is apparent. Keegan walked me home, hugged me tightly, and left so that Trevor could come over. All he said was 'call me if you need me and don't be a stranger.' Saying that it breaks my heart a bit that he handles this so well would be an understatement. Placing my art out along the walls, there is a knock at the door.

Opening it, I don't have a chance to react before I'm being kissed. The door closes behind me and I'm kissing him back. My mind is spinning, feeling every touch and every movement. My shirt is over my head and on the floor next to me; I'm struggling to undo his pants as he unhooks my bra. Sliding his pants off, I grab him, pulling him to me. Grabbing the hem of his

Gracie Wilson

shirt, I lift it over his head and his lips find mine again. He takes my bottom lip in between his teeth, biting softly, causing me to moan unexpectedly. He begins undoing my jeans and I shimmy them down my legs.

    He brings his hand around to the back of my neck and places his other one just above my bottom, holding me to him. Guiding me back, we find the bed, falling into it. Slowly I bring my fingers to the top of his boxers and begin pulling them down. He kicks them off and then does the same thing to my panties, bringing them down around my ankles. I slide them off and bring my hands up and along his back. The sexual tension is finally having an outlet. He closes the space between us, not even leaving an inch. I feel him press against me and I allow him, pulling myself closer to his body. He continues looking right into my eyes, making sure this is everything I've wanted. Right now, I can't think of anything I'd want more than to be doing this with him.

Chapter Twenty-Six

"What does this mean?" He asks as we rush putting our clothes back on. "Becca, what does this mean?" Looking at him, I wish I had the answers he wants but I just can't figure this out.

"I don't know, Jake." I feel the emotions of what just happened set in.

"Becca." Frustration builds up.

"JAKE! I don't know, okay? I have no idea what any of this means." My phone beeps and I rush to it.

'I'll be there in fifteen minutes-Trevor'

"Was that him?" Jake asks quietly.

"If by him you mean Trevor, then yes. He will be here in fifteen minutes.

"Becca, please just talk to me." Turning from Jake, I find myself torn between what just happened and what should be happening. This wasn't what I planned.

"Jake, I don't know what to say any more. You just get angry. You were horrible to me tonight. The things you said. Then you show up here and you are just asking me 'what does this mean?' Why can't you tell me that? My brain is tired of trying to think through this mess." Turning back to Jake, I can see him working through everything I've just said.

"It means you have a choice. You can stand by me; deal with the fact that Sarah might be having my child. Not give up on us. You could choose to love me unconditionally. The way I love you. But the choice is yours, Becca, it always has been."

"Am I allowed to say I don't know? Is that wrong?" I whisper, in response.

"No, the only thing wrong was how I treated you tonight. I was jealous, seeing him connect with you over art. To top it off, I didn't know anything about him. I know that's my fault because I was so distant from you this summer. It's no excuse." Jake's words sink in and I find myself wishing someone other than me were making this choice.

"Becca, I have to leave. I won't make this worse for you by having him show up with me here." I'm thankful for this because if my life got any more complicated I'd be finding the first plane out of this city. "That being said, I am jealous. Jealous of the way he gets you. Of what he wants from you, of all the things he can give you that I can't. But know this. He can't love you like me.

The Broken Girl

Nobody can." Jake kisses me, pressing his lips firmly against mine, and just like he appeared, he's gone.

Standing in the middle of my room, I am in a state of shock. What did I just do? Jake was right. What does this mean? Before I have time to react to anything, my door is being knocked on and I open it cautiously.

"Rebecca."

I open it wide waving Trevor in. "Find it alright?"

He nods. "The girls down the hall were helpful. Nicky and Lily say hello." Of course they do. I mentally make a note to tell them of the newest drama I've added to my life.

Trevor begins pacing around, looking at my walls that are currently papered in my art. "Rebecca, I'm glad I came. I was right about you."

"What are you talking about?" I ask him quietly. "Rebecca, you are an amazing artist. You have a keen eye, with attention to detail. All the things that will make you very successful and I wouldn't be much of a business man if I didn't try to grasp that talent when I have the chance." I'm still lost as to his thoughts. My work is okay, but I'm just starting out. "My offer at the firm is very much true. I'd like you to take a few weeks to talk about it with your family, and any friends you feel would benefit you from their wisdom. I'm opening an art-dealing firm. My first task is to talk this artist into commissioning a few pieces."

"Trevor, I'm not ready to negotiate and do dealings. I'm just starting my second year of schooling and it's not in art or marketing."

He chuckles, looking closely at my piece I'd painted before coming to visit here almost two years ago. During the summer, I'd worked on it more closely and defined some things. I'd labelled it 'The Broken Girl.'

"Rebecca, I'm afraid I need your help. The only person who can get this artist is you." Walking to Trevor's side, I look, trying to see what he's seeing that is causing him to have this huge smile. "That artist is you, Rebecca."

Wait, me? "You want me to help with the firm and paint?"

He nods.

"That seems a little good to be true, so what else would you expect of me?" I've had too many things go wrong on me. I'm not jumping into this.

"Rebecca, as much as I wish you were ready, you are not. Right now, all you can offer me is your talent, your knowledge, and your appreciation of art. I understand that more than you know. So think about it. I've also made the option of showing one of your pieces. I'd like to borrow this one for the occasion." Looking around at my paintings I try and imagine them covering the walls of a gallery, although it's hard. I'd never thought I'd have this chance, or this type of future. He's pointing to the painting I'd been working on so hard this summer and I'm happy that it's one of my better pieces.

"Trevor, I will definitely think about this. As for the painting…what the heck, right? If you say it's good, who am I to say otherwise?" He claps his hands together as if he's already succeeded in getting me to work for him. Agreeing to let him take my painting already has my body in a panic.

"Lovely, now I've already had my assistant pick up a dress for you. Your flight leaves at seven in the morning, so you'd better start packing. You leave in seven hours. It's time for Rebecca Potts to stop hiding."

***

There are cameras flashing and I haven't even stepped out of the limo yet. Trevor looks at me and puts his hand over mine, trying to help my nerves. It only further panics me. It pulls me back to reality. In a few minutes, I will be stepping out of this car and I'm going to be out there for the world to see.

"Trevor, this wasn't such a good idea." I am hoping he will agree and let me go home.

"Rebecca, if I didn't think you could handle this I would never have brought you. Not only are you an amazing model but an exceptionally gifted artist." The doors to the limo open, Trevor gets out, and holds out a hand for me to grab. I emerge from the limo and the flashes start. Trevor puts his arm around my waist and guides me through and into the gallery.

This place is enormous; there are paintings everywhere, and people covering every spot, looking at the art. Trevor continues bringing us through the crowd and eventually lands in front of the portrait he painted of me. People are looking at it and saying how beautiful it is. If only they knew how broken that person really is. How confusing her life has gotten.

"Rebecca, I'm going to go meet up with the host and talk about my speech. Are you okay?" He looks at me and I nod, still staring at a painting of myself.

"Beautiful." I gasp at the sound of his voice.

The Broken Girl

"It really is beautiful." I respond, bringing myself down memory lane.

"Yes, the portrait is beautiful too." Turning, I stand there looking at my mystery man.

"Jake." He brings me to him in a hug and I let him.

"Becca, fancy meeting you here." I laugh at his attempt to brush this off.

"You know, I've already had one stalking boyfriend, and I'm not sure if I'm looking to make it two."

He gets a huge infectious grin on his face. "Boyfriend, huh?"

I elbow him and he just laughs harder. "Jake, really, what are you doing here?"

"Becca, you thought the first time your work is going to be shown that I wouldn't drop everything to be here?" If only it were that easy, or could it be?

"Well, thank you. I'm nervous and want to crawl under a rock, but I wouldn't be Becca if I didn't feel that way."

He brings me to him, holding my hand. "No, you wouldn't be my Becca if you didn't feel that way." My heart warms and I wonder if I could really make it this easy. Just choose Jake, forget everything, and be happy.

"Well, this must be the beautiful Becca you never stopped talking about." Turning around, I see a man who looks just like Jake, just twenty-five years older.

"She is everything you said she was." He is looking at me with such kind eyes and Jake follows suit. I'm wearing a long black satin dress with a small train at the back of it and it has a loose neckline. I'm wearing silver high heels and a simple silver heart necklace.

"She's more really," Jake adds.

"Well, where are my manners? My name is Jared Kelso. As I'm sure you've gathered, I'm Jake's dad." I step forward, giving him a quick hug. I laugh at the fact that I just hugged him.

"Sorry, I'm sure a handshake would have worked too."

He laughs. "Ah, yes but then you wouldn't be the woman my son has spent the last year and a half talking about. It's nice to finally meet you, Becca. I've heard nothing but amazing things about you."

Trevor doesn't come back, so I continue talking with Jake and his dad. They are two of a kind. It's easy, just like it always was with Jake. Two people approach us and they both look at Jake and his father. Jake places his arm around my waist and pulls me towards him, almost protectively.

The Broken Girl

"There you two are. We've been looking for you, and who is this?" I assume this must be Jake's mom. She's beautiful, of course, but Jake is a double of his dad.

"Dear, this is Jake's girlfriend, Becca." Jakes dad is beaming. "She's one of the models of the portraits being showcased and even has her own painting being displayed.

"I didn't know you were with anyone, Jake. Must not be anything important enough to tell your sister." She says.

Jake's dad glares at her. "That was very rude, Denise. Don't say such things. Becca is all your brother every speaks about. I feel like I already know her." He smiles and my mood picks up after his sister's outburst.

"Don't mind my sister. She's just mad that she couldn't pawn me off to one of her friends." I laugh nervously.

"Well, Becky, is it?" With that name, my whole body goes rigid. Flashes of Dillon come back and I know I need to get out of here.

"It's Becca, mom." Jake says loudly.

"If you all will excuse me, I have something I need to take care of."

Making my way away from all of them, I find myself in a hall trying to calm down. I should be able to hear that name. It's over, he's dead, and he can't hurt me anymore.

~ 252 ~

"Becca, Becca." I hear Jake calling my name and I know from the tone he's worried.

"I'm over here, Jake."

My phone beeps and I check it. *'I know he's with you. Stay away from them. They will never choose you over their child.'*

Quickly I reply to her, asking which of the many possibilities was she referring to, and I delete the message. Jake races up to me, places his hands on either side of my face. He kisses me passionately and I allow myself to have this, to have Jake.

"I love you, Jake. I still love you more than you will ever know," I say, as soon as he releases the hold he had on my lips.

"Becca, you have no idea how long I've been waiting to hear you say those words. I love you too, more than I ever thought possible. I won't let anything come between us, Becca. I've lost you once. I won't lose you again."

Placing my lips softly against his, I kiss him again, just because I can. "So girlfriend, eh?" I say, with a smirk on my face.

"I told you, nobody can love you like I can." He begins kissing me again and I give in, letting him have all of me. His phone rings, interrupting us. He doesn't answer it and as soon as it stops, it just starts up again.

"Hello… okay… yes, I know… I'll be right there." He hangs up the phone and

The Broken Girl

looks at me with sadness in his eyes. "I have to go." My mind isn't on the same page and I'm confused as to what just happened.

"Who was it?" I ask.

"It was Sarah, and she needs me. She thinks something's wrong with the baby." Jake is looking at me, hoping I'll understand. I don't because, of course, nothing is wrong. She's just doing what she does best. Screw up my life.

"Jake, she's fine. She messaged me telling me to stay away from you. She's just doing this to hurt us, so don't let her."

Grabbing my phone, I call Alec. "Hey, it's me. Can you go check on Sarah? She called telling Jake she thinks something is wrong with the baby... Thanks." Hanging up my phone, Jake is glaring at me.

"What?" I ask, but I know he's mad.

"She called me, and she needs me, not Alec." I push off the wall and start pacing around him.

"Jake, if she was that worried why would she call the one person who isn't even in the same city? She's doing this to get in between us. Why hasn't she taken the paternity test? Because she knows it will end this game." He looks at me and I've never seen him look at me this way.

"That could be my child, Becca. I'm sorry that you can't understand that she's scared and isn't ready. I don't have time for this right now so we will talk about this later." He starts walking off.

"No, we won't! I'm supposed to be your 'girlfriend,' aren't I? If that's true, stay with me and let my brother check on her. If something is wrong, fine. We will go together because that's the only way this works." He's shaking his head and I feel defeated.

"Even if there isn't something wrong, she needs me." That pisses me off and I lose what little grip I had on my anger.

"I need you! You know what tonight means to me. I'm your girlfriend, not her!"

"Not anymore," he says, as he pulls away from me.

"Jake, if you walk away now, that's it. I won't compete with her."

He walks away.

Chapter Twenty-Seven

"Rebecca, there you are. We are going up now." Trevor looks at me and I feel like he can see everything that's just happened. Trevor guides me back into the gallery and we pass Jake who's talking to his dad. They are arguing and I wish I could hear what about but I'm being brought up on stage.

"Please welcome Trevor Hunt and Rebecca Potts," the announcer says and everyone claps, causing my nerves to get the better of me. Trevor steps in front of the microphone and begins talking. My eyes never leave Jake, watching him so closely that my eyes feel like they aren't blinking. His dad is looking at me and pointing. He's angry. Jake isn't backing down though. "I'd like you all to welcome Becca Potts."

Trevor moves aside letting me take the stage. Before my nerves get the better of me, I step up. "As Trevor said, my name is Rebecca Potts. Behind me, to the left, is my portrait that Trevor painted. To the right of me is a painting I did myself. It's labelled

Gracie Wilson

The Broken Girl. I was asked to speak about the piece and its meanings." My eyes find Jake and he's watching me. "I began working on this just after my seventeenth birthday. During the course of the next year and a half, I continued to work on it. Define it. Breaking it down inch by inch to bring every emotion possible to the painting. Each tear you see pictured here isn't that just of a brush and paint. It's of tragedy and losses. My tragedies, my losses. But those defined the painting. They brought it to life. Gave it reality. The broken can rise again, but not with those who break them."

I pause for a moment. Jake turns, leaving. His dad tries to stop him but it's no use. Jake leaves, walking right out the front door with his mother and sister trailing behind.

"Life is full of loss. It makes a person, builds a picture. Each artist in this room builds off some emotion when they paint. Sometimes those emotions are so raw that the picture comes out like mine has. Full of a voice." The crowd claps and I decide right then and there what I'm doing.

"I'd like to thank the gallery and Trevor Hunt for his guidance. I'd also like to take this opportunity to accept his job offer and the work that he's asked me to commission." The room erupts in applause. Everyone but

The Broken Girl

Jake's dad joins in; he wears those same sad eyes I've seen so many times on Jake.

"Rebecca, that's marvellous. I will get started right away," Trevor says, once we leave the stage.

"Trevor, please don't tell anyone yet. I need to tell my brother and my parents." Mentally I make note that I need to tell Keegan but I know that's just going to hurt.

"Rebecca, I know your parents won't be excited that you will be leaving school. I will pay for your education and make sure it is the finest I can find. Rest assured, Rebecca, those who work for me are taken care of." I smile and nod.

"Can I have a word, Becca?" Turning, I see Jake's dad waiting for me.

"Mr. Kelso, I was going to come say goodbye before I left." I lied, so sue me.

"Becca, I don't know what's going on but I hope that it wasn't what made you decide to take this offer." Just like Jake, his dad can see through me but he's only part right.

"No, sir, it wasn't the only factor. I've been spending my summers abroad, studying art and before returning home, I looked into schooling over there. It's the best move for me right now. My brother will be graduating this year and then I will be there alone anyway. I've always wanted to study art and it is my true passion." I hope this explanation will suffice.

"Well, I can see that you're extremely talented. You're everything my son has said you are and more, actually. I thought you were this mythical woman that he'd made up because I just couldn't believe that someone like you existed. Now I'm afraid he's ruining that. My son is my world, but maybe he doesn't deserve such an accomplished person. Becca, wherever you go I have a feeling you will have all you've wanted. For my son's sake, I hope he pulls his head out of his ass and figures that out quickly." I break out laughing and Jake's dad does the same.

"Mr. Kelso…"

He interrupts me. "Jared."

I nod and continue. "Jared, can you please not tell him about this? I will when the time is right, but I just need to tell my brother and my family first. Work everything out first and then let Jake know the plan."

He thinks for a moment, then agrees. "It's not my place to tell him when if he'd only waited five minutes longer, he could have celebrated with you. Good luck, Becca, I hope to see you again soon." He gives me

The Broken Girl

a hug and leaves me there with so many questions going on in my head.

***

I don't return home for two days. Trevor and I had so many things to get ready for my departure. I've called my parents and they reluctantly agreed. Trevor is hard to resist. I have to admit if I hadn't been sold on the idea, his speech would have done it for me too. My parents agreed to let me tell Alec and they are somewhat happy. My mother was more receptive. All my dad was concerned about was not finishing at Lakehead.

When I get back to the dorms, I don't know what I was expecting but Charlotte and Drake waiting for me was not it.

"I'm leaving." I blurt it out without thinking it through.

"You just got back?" Charlotte says, confused.

"No, Charlotte, I'm leaving, as in I won't be finishing at Lakehead. My parents already know. I have been offered a job, commissioned artwork, and a full education in art along with anything else I want. I've already accepted it." Charlotte stops for a second and I see her working through everything.

"When do we leave?" I'm shaking my head, but Drake intercepts this conversation.

"Well, I can't leave until Christmas break, but I can transfer anywhere after that."

"That was not what I was expecting you to say, Drake." He just smiles at me.

"Drake... you'd follow us?" Charlotte asks softly.

"Becca needs you, and I need you. It's that simple. I love you, Charlotte." She kisses him and I am so happy that they've found each other and that we have each other because I know they are going to be all I have very soon.

"Well, I guess I will tell Trevor I need a bigger place, unless you don't want to be my roommates?" They both hug me tightly and we laugh.

"Wait, what are you doing here?" They both shuffle their feet and don't respond.

"What is it?"

Drake looks at Charlotte and she just shakes her head.

"Okay, I will tell you. Everyone is waiting for us over at the house. After Jake got back and found that Sarah was fine, he demanded a test. He had them fast tracked, and it cost a fortune but they are back. It's time to find out who's the father of the baby, Becca."

The Broken Girl

I haven't said anything since they told me; I just nodded and followed them. I now find myself sitting in my brother's house.

"Becca…" Jake comes up to me.

"I don't want to hear it right now, Jake. Let's just get this over with, okay?"

Charlotte has been allocated to read the results. I watch as she pulls out a page. "Keegan, you are not the father." Looking at Keegan, he gets up and comes right to me. He kisses me lightly.

"Thank you for being there for me, Bec." I feel awful because he doesn't know about Jake or about me leaving.

"Jake, you're not the father either." I watch as the realization hits Jake.

"Alec, you are the father of Sarah's child. I'm sorry," she says and Sarah screams.

"This is rigged! No way."

"Guess that lifetime of misery is going to start now. Sarah, why don't you tell everyone that you did this all to get back at me." She screams again and I put my hands over my eyes.

"It had to be the brother, it couldn't be the boyfriends! Seriously, I slept with Alec because he was hot and I was getting even."

I just shake my head. "You really are that screwed up, Sarah," I say and turn away, grabbing my bag.

"Becca, where are you going?" Jake asks.

"Well, since I know my brother is the father, that's all I really needed from this conversation. I'm going to go call a lawyer and figure out how I can make sure my niece or nephew never has to deal with someone who only brought them into this world to get back at someone." I know in reality there isn't much I can do but it's nice to say that.

Walking out of the house, I finally feel free. Instead of waiting for someone to walk with me home, I just decide to walk alone. My mind starts thinking about all the things I need to do and all the packing I need to do. Not to mention telling Alec I'm leaving. It's dark and I love the peacefulness of the streets. I see headlights coming from behind me and I turn just in time to see that they are headed straight for me.

"BEC!!! WATCH OUT!"

Chapter Twenty-Eight

There is smoke coming from the car that has hit a tree. My ears are ringing and I feel light. Like at any minute I might blow away. Hands come around me and I can't seem to get my eyes to focus.

"Bec!" Keegan says loudly. "Bec, can't you hear me?" I nod and my head feels wet. "You are bleeding, Bec, let me look." Keegan lightly touches my forehead and I wince. "It looks fine." Everything that just happen registers and I get up, running around to the driver.

Sarah is lying there and I open the door, pulling her from the car carefully. "Keegan, help me." He helps me guide her down.

"I couldn't even hit you right." My hands fly up to my mouth. She had done this on purpose.

"I let your crazy boyfriend into your dorm, told him when you were getting off the plane, and even went as far as leaving threatening messages. What will it take to kill you?" Her words are slurring and

Gracie Wilson

Keegan is trying to pull me away from her. I look down and I see that there is blood soaking her pants.

"Keegan get help, the baby." I say as quickly as possible. Keegan looks at me. "Get help, Keegan." He leaves and Sarah tries to move but she isn't able to do much more then twist.

> "You won." With that, her eyes go into the back of her head and she goes limp. "SOMEBODY HELP ME!"

***

Standing in the waiting room, being on the other end of those doors, and not knowing what is happening, I now know what I've put everyone through. They rushed Sarah in as soon as the paramedics got her here. They went into surgery and we've been waiting here. The doors push open and a doctor approaches us.

"Are you the family?" he asks.

"No, I'm the father of the child," my brother says.

"We rushed her into surgery but we couldn't stop the bleeding. She had lost too much blood and was hemorrhaging. We were able to perform an emergency Caesarean, but that only further

The Broken Girl

compromised her care. At that point, we focused on the baby as there wasn't anything we could do for her."

My brother is barely holding on and I grab his hand supportively. "Doctor, was the baby okay?" Not that I wanted this or want to think about this, but I know my brother does. He's wondering if he just lost another part of this family.

"Your son is still very small but he is healthy. We will keep him until he is up on his weight. Once he's clear to go home, we will release him to you." I nod as my brother stands there, and I'm not even sure if he has heard anything the doctor has said.

"I'm so sorry for your loss. The nurses will come around to take you to your son." The doctor goes to walk away but turns around. "What is his name?" I look up, never thinking my brother would have to do this all on his own.

"Michael Potts." Just like that, my brother is a father, and already one I'm envious of.

Everyone is quiet and no one is talking. A nurse comes up and smiles at us. "I can take you in to meet your son now and one other person."

Alec gets up and starts walking before looking back at me. "Becca, I can't do this without you." I quickly get up and catch up to my brother, putting my hand in his.

"Thank God you don't have to, right?" He smiles softly and we walk into the nursery area. There are little button noses everywhere.

When we see the label Michael Potts, we both stop. "You can do this, Alec." He lets go of me and walks up to where his son is lying. The nurse picks him up and puts him in my brother's arms. As soon as I see this, the tears begin to stream down my face. My brother is crying, holding his son, and they are all alone. No mom, just us. Michael is beautiful; he has my brother's eyes and his mouth. Sarah's hair color and nose; that's all he will ever get from his mother.

"Alec, I have to tell you something?"

"Becca, I'm so sorry about everything. I never should have made you come here."

I place my arm on him, stopping him. "Alec, I was offered a job. I was going to drop out and go to school in Europe. Mom and Dad already know."

He smiles at me. Not the reaction I was thinking I'd be getting. "Becca that's amazing."

"Alec, I can't go, you both need me. I won't leave you when you need me the most." My brother walks up to me, placing Michael in my arms.

The Broken Girl

"Becca, I told you not to stay out of guilt. Besides that, I would never hold you back from this." Looking down at my nephew, I just want to protect him from everything in the world. "I know that look, Becca. I have that same look when I look at you. You are going to be an amazing aunt. One who lives in Europe and we visit regularly. Who sends all sorts of funny outfits and paints his nursery. But you are going to be an aunt who lives her life. The way she should. It's always been art, Becca. Always. I want Michael to be able to be whatever makes him happy. We have to show him that."

My brother had instantly turned into a father and I became an aunt. "Mom will be on the first plane and she will have no problem staying until I finish school. You were always meant for more than just this, Becca, whether that's being painted or painting. As long as you're happy, we will be happy for you," Alec says, as he brings his finger along the face of his son.

Alec had to deal with paperwork so he let me bring the baby out to see everyone once the nurse cleared him. When I walk out to the waiting room, they all stand up, looking at me.

"Everyone, this is Michael Potts, my nephew." Charlotte is the first to steal the baby from me. Her and Drake just sit there, staring at the baby with so much love on their faces.

Jake hasn't done much and is just sitting in the corner. "Jake, I know you wanted to be the dad. I'm sorry," I say, and he just looks up at me.

"I just wanted someone that needed me."

"People need you, Jake. I've met your family and they love you. You are needed. Alec is going to need all of us for this. Yes, you can't be the dad. But you can be one amazing uncle." Charlotte brings the baby over and places him back in my arms.

Jake is watching him so closely. "Yes, I will be the coolest uncle."

We hear a chuckle and look up. "Second coolest." Keegan is standing in front of us with a huge grin.

"No, fools, you both suck. I will be the coolest uncle because I'm going to be living with his coolest cousin and aunty." I freeze at Drake's words and he look up at me once he realizes what he's done.

"What are you talking about?" Jake asks.

"Well, Alec is going to need more space so we will give him our room. Becca can't live in the dorms forever. Only makes sense

The Broken Girl

that we all move in together." He is trying to cover up his mishap.

"Well, then I guess it's settled," I say, putting the biggest smile on my face I can manage. Keegan hasn't said anything. He's just watching me.

I hand the baby over to Jake and he looks lost. "Just support his head. I'll be right back."

Walking over, I get Keegan's attention and ask him to follow me. "Keegan," I say, because I feel like I should just tell him now.

"No, whatever it is, I don't want to know." He starts to walk away from me, leaving the waiting room.

"Don't." I beg him to stay and he whips around on me. His face is flooded with unspoken emotions. I thought that if I told Keegan he would want to come, or at least have the possibility of seeing each other, but from what I see my heart stands no chance here.

"Keegan, do you blame me for Sarah?" I never thought about it until now but out of everyone, Keegan was the one that actually had feelings for Sarah. He just turns to walk away from me again. "Keegan please don't go."

"Don't you get it? I don't want to be here with you." Keegan yells at me. I flinch and watch him walk away.

I gather myself before returning to the others. They are all staring at me and this is the last thing I can deal with. "Well, time to get this baby back to his daddy," I say, and I leave them all to say goodbye.

Alec is waiting for me when I get back; he's looking out the window as if it holds the answers he's looking for. "Your phone rang so I answered it. It was Trevor," Alec says.

"Oh, what did he want?" I ask, questioningly.

"He said he was able to get a bigger place arranged for you and your cousin." I take a deep breath, ready for a fight. "I'm so happy that Charlotte is going with you, because that means Drake won't be far behind."

I laugh at my brother's mention of Drake. "Yeah, you are right about that."

"What about Jake and Keegan?" he asks.

"I wish I knew, but all I can think is that some distance might be just what we all need." He nods and continues looking out the window.

"Do they know?" Walking over to Alec, I wish I knew what to say.

The Broken Girl

"I'm not going to tell them. Once I'm already gone, they will understand. They will just try to stop me."

"How soon can you leave, Becca?"

Chapter Twenty-Nine

When I get back to the dorms I walk into my hall and stop. Keegan is sitting against my door. When he sees me, he rushes up to his feet.

"Keegan." I say acknowledging him.

"Bec, can we talk?" He looks so badly broken and I begin wonder if all this has finally weighed on him.

"Of course." I unlock my door and wave him in. Looking around, some of my art is still taking up residence on my walls. Keegan is just wandering around as if he's looking for something.

"Keegan, I'm so sorry about everything. This is all so crazy. I don't blame you for being angry with me about Sarah's death." He just looks at me like he's trying to figure out exactly how to break it to me.

"Bec, I was upset about Sarah and blaming you for her death. But I know now that she came after you; I heard all the things she'd done. Everything that happened: with Dillon, the threatening notes,

The Broken Girl

and of course, the drugs. Then trying to run you over. What happened to Sarah was at her own hands, and I don't want you carrying that guilt with you."

I don't understand his answer. "Why didn't you want to be there with me then, Keegan?" I ask, trying to figure out what is going on in his poor head.

"I didn't want to be there with you because I feel like you just fucking suck me into you. I feel myself gravitate to you and it's fucking with my head. It's screwing with me because I'm trying so hard just to be your friend, but every nerve in my body is screaming at me, telling me to love you, to make you let me be in love with you. Being just your friend is making it that much worse because I still love you." I don't respond to his words. I can't. My heart is breaking and beating with happiness simultaneously because I know it doesn't change anything.

"Please remember me, Keegan. You have always been there for me. I want you to remember everything and all those times. I want to be able to be there for you," I say, knowing if he remembers all the good and bad times, he'd agree that space is what we need.

"You're beautiful, amazing, and everything I could ever ask for. Losing my memory was the best thing that ever happened to me. It gave me you, in a new way; you were able to help build me into the man I've become. A man worthy of you, Bec." His words are like spurts of electricity trying to jumpstart my heart. It would be easy to just stay here with Keegan in our own little bubble. The problem with that is there is always reality just on the other side, bursting to get in. It always does too; we can't hide from the world. That doesn't change the fact that tonight I've fallen in love with Keegan all over again.

"I'm sorry for blaming you, Keegan. All I've done is hurt myself by hurting you. I'm done feeling that way." No truer words have ever been spoken. I feel like this is exactly the way I can describe my feeling to Keegan. I'm ready to tell him and to let him know I'm leaving but he interrupts me.

"We were always meant to say goodbye, weren't we?" His words are my undoing. I grab him and bring him right down on top of me, onto my bed, kissing him eagerly. He is meeting me pace for pace. Giving it his all. Like he knows this was always meant to be.

"God, you are so beautiful." His words free me of any embarrassment or hesitation. I pull my own shirt off, causing him to be distracted at the sight of my scar. As much as I hate it, this reminds me of my time with

The Broken Girl

Jake. When I try to move his hands away, he does something that Jake never did. Instead of telling me I'm still beautiful, he says the words I need to hear.

"Don't, Bec. Don't you ever be ashamed of your scar. It means you were stronger than whatever tried to hurt you. Tried to take you away from us." Staring into Keegan's eyes, there isn't anyone else I'd rather be with. No one has ever made me feel so accepted, and no one has seen me in such a true light. "Please say we haven't lost us."

My fingers lace with his and I bring one of his hands over my heart. "Never, Keegan." He brings his lips softly against mine, gentle and lovingly. Making sure I feel his love with every kiss. My patience begins to waver and so does his. We are both soon grasping at each other's clothing, pulling them off. In seconds, we are both naked. He's holding his weight off me and I wish this was how our first time could've been.

"We get a do over, Bec. We get to have this again. If you will let us." His words are exactly what I was thinking, showing how in sync we have become since the accident. If I had met this Keegan, would there have ever been a question of whom I belonged with?

Gracie Wilson

Using my hands and my weight, I roll him so I'm straddling him. "I love you, Keegan Keller." Those words are all I can get out right now.

"I know what you're going to do, Bec. Just know that I'll always be right here waiting for you. Whenever you are ready, just say the word. I don't deserve you, Bec, but I'm asking that you let me have you anyway?" Keegan whispers.

Bringing my mouth down on his, there's nothing between us. We are connected in every way. Our movements are matched and effortless. Like no two people were better suited to share this. His body presses hard against mine and I feel the movements of his hips. He places his hands around my waist and turns us so he's on top of me, looking down into my eyes. He thrusts and I feel myself getting closer. His grip on me tightens and I know he's not far behind. We continue like this, working each other, showing the love that our words couldn't even begin to express.

Just as my body is ready to give in to the pleasure he's giving to my body, he speaks. "I love you, Becca."

Those words are all I needed to get to my climax and he follows me. We lay there, our bodies exhausted. After a few minutes, he leans over and grabs something from his

The Broken Girl

pants. It's the locket that he gave me for Christmas; I'd given it back to him.

"I need you to have this. I know you think me falling in love with you now is crazy. Let me be crazy. I'm sorry for all those nights that I may never remember. You put your entire world on hold for me. My heart needs you to have the world." I nod and he does the latch, placing the necklace back around my neck.

"Where it belongs," he says, as he runs his finger along the chain. I turn, snuggling into him. Getting my fill of Keegan is never going to happen but I will take everything I can get.

"I could hold you in my arms forever and it still wouldn't be long enough." Somehow Keegan knows this is goodbye. I just never thought I'd feel this way when I realized it too. We lay there until I can hear the birds through my window. I know that we've had this bubble, our bubble, but the world is bursting in, causing us to have to face reality.

Once Keegan is deeply asleep, I go to get dressed and grab a few of my things, knowing I'm doing the right thing. But my heart is still breaking every minute I'm not in that bed with him. I give into my wants and go back to him.

Gracie Wilson

"You will think I have moved on, and you will fall in love with someone else. I'm in love with you and always will be. Which is why this is goodbye. I'm setting you free, Keegan. Just be happy. I love you." I lean down and kiss him softly, careful not to wake him. I gather up my things and sneak out into the night and right out of Keegan's life. Leaving one final note for him.

I will always love you, Keegan. You gave me the best of everything but sometimes that's just not enough. You deserve more than I can give you. I want you to move on, so do this for me. Be happy. Love without fear.

I'm already gone, so please don't look for me.

Your Bec, Always <3

Chapter Thirty

Walking into the airport, I can't help the déjà vu I feel. Airports have become my second home since coming to Lakehead. Waiting for my flight that will bring me into Toronto to get onto my next flight with Trevor, I'm wondering if I'm making the right decision. My heart is hesitating. Looking around, I am in complete shock when I see those sliding doors open and Jake walking in. I haven't called anyone; no one knows I'm leaving right now. He walks right up to me, giving nothing away as to why he is here.

"Jake, what are you doing here?" Once the words are out my heart comes to a realization. I care. When I'm with Keegan, he is all I see. When I'm with Jake, he's all I see. I love them both, which is why my choice to leave is the right one. "My dad called. When I told him everything about Sarah, he told me I had to see you. I didn't know what he meant. So I came over but I saw you letting Keegan in. I waited but, well, you know how long you were in there and what you were doing." My whole face pales at this.

"I waited, watching. I saw you put your bag in a cab and I knew then. You're running away again, Becca." I go to say something, anything, but he puts his hand up, stopping me.

"You are just like Sarah. The only difference is you couldn't sleep with Alec because he's your brother." His words are filled with disgust. I slap him in the middle of this airport. I know he's hurting, if he'd only admit that. But right now all he feels is rage. So I let him have his words, for now. If only you could change and I'd stay the same. But all you do is push me the fuck away. I'm done trying, Becca.

"Jake, it's not like that. I think this is what we need. What we all need. I have an amazing opportunity to work with my art. If anyone would understand that, it is you." He is shaking his head. I know nothing I'm saying is sinking in.

"Becca, art isn't a future. It's a hobby. It's time to grow up." I fight back my tears. He doesn't deserve them. What I told Drake was true. Being in love shouldn't hurt this much.

"Jake, I know you are just mad and you don't mean it. You are just angry about my

The Broken Girl

choices. But they are my choices. I love you, Jake, and I know you still love me." I say this to him, hoping that out of this whole conversation he will at least absorb those words.

"I don't love you, Becca, not anymore." His words cut me so deep I wish I was anywhere but here.

"You are just saying this because you're angry, and you will regret this, Jacob!" I tell him.

"No. I don't, Becca." He doesn't look sorry. Jake looks at me like this is a chore.

"Jake, you promised me you'd never lie to me, so please don't start now," I say, with my voice shaking.

"I'm not lying to you, Becca. The only promise I've made that I'm breaking was saying I'd always be there for you. Because I won't." I am looking for any hint of him lying, but I can't find any of his tells. Not that he's ever lied to me before. This isn't the Jake I knew.

"Jake, please. Don't do this to me, Jake. I love you. This isn't about me running this is about me doing what I want to with my art. That doesn't change anything. I need you. I love you, and you're still my best friend who loves his best friend!" I beg.

"It's time you find another best friend."

Gracie Wilson

Just like that, I know that leaving was the absolute right choice. There is too much damage here with Keegan and Jake. There is too much water under the bridge to move forward right now.

"I don't want to see you, or be with you. I just wanted you to know you are not running away, because there's nothing left here for you to run from." With each word, my thoughts of our someday are vanishing. Jake is throwing in the towel on us.

"Have a good life, Becca." He turns, walking out of the same door he had only just come through, leaving me alone.

Instead of doing what 'Becca' usually would and fall to the floor at the loss of Jake, I turned and boarded my plane. It wasn't about fight or flight. It was about survival. I'm fighting this time, but I won't fight for someone who doesn't want me in his or her life. I will fight for me. For my future with my art, and for the Becca I have become. I won't continue to be the shell of the girl I was. I'm done being *lonely* and *broken*. I'm leaving and I'm never coming back. It's time for me to become *missing*.

Epilogue

Becca

Standing in the room, I pace. How did this happen?

"Charlotte, what am I going to do if I'm right?" I say, hoping my cousin will have some wise words of wisdom.

"You will deal. You're not the same girl you were when you left Thunder Bay."

I left my home, family, Jake, and Keegan, three months ago. I left without notice, telling few where I actually am. Those who do know where I am aren't telling anyone. I needed this.

At the time, everyone thought I was being overzealous, but the change and success I've had has shown everyone that I can be the person I want to be without needing to be taken care of. I just hope that for once I'm wrong. That I won't be tested on how strong I really have become and far I've come. I still have so much I want to do, but this might change that.

"It's time," Charlotte says.
Looking down, I read the word that has just changed my entire life.
Pregnant.

THE END

The Broken Girl

Look for Gracie in the trees enjoying nature's wonders, traveling to see the latest animal conservations, or at aquariums all around the world. This girl loves nature and all animals. She has many pets and is always adding new additions. The more the merrier in her mind. Sitting under the shade reading a book, letting the world around her pass by, while she is safe in her bubble of imagination. Well that is where she'd love to stay. She is a softball player, can be talked into the occasional Karaoke and loves going out to dance. She is a first generation Canadian living in Ontario. Her family is from Scotland, so finding her in the hot sun for very long is unlikely, but give her rain and thunderstorms and she's golden.

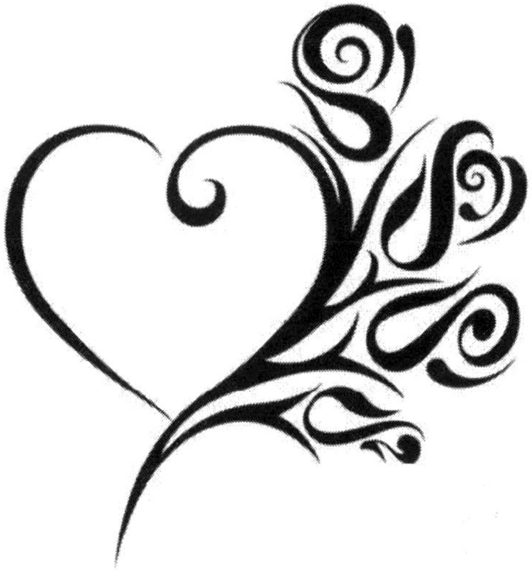

Made in the USA
San Bernardino, CA
16 March 2016